W

Jessica's marriage to Matt Fenwood had
foundered on the rock of her ambition
to make a success of her career as a T.V.
director—and it was a dreadful shock
when he suddenly turned up again and
she found herself forced to work with
him. It had taken her four years to get
this man out of her system; could she be
sure she had got him out for ever?

WILDTRACK

BY

NICOLA WEST

MILLS & BOON LIMITED
15–16 BROOK'S MEWS
LONDON W1A 1DR

First published 1983
Australian copyright 1983
Philippine copyright 1984
This edition 1984

© Nicola West 1983

ISBN 0 263 74470 1

Set in Monophoto Times 10 on 10½ pt.
01-0184 – 60837

Made and printed in Great Britain by
Richard Clay (The Chaucer Press) Ltd,
Bungay, Suffolk

For
JANE JACKSON

CHAPTER ONE

THERE was a pleasant hum of activity in the offices of Mercia TV. as Jessica Fenwood pushed open the swing doors at the end of the corridor. She stood still for a moment, taking in the scene—the desks scattered around the big open-plan room, the burble of voices from those using phones or grouped around the conversation area in the middle. New projects being discussed, old ones analysed; a tiny thrill ran through her as she wondered just what this new producer had in mind for her. A documentary subject that was right up her street, Hilary had told her when she phoned, but she'd refused to say any more. 'You'll have to come in to find out,' she'd told Jessica firmly, and so here Jessica was.

Hilary was at her desk, riffling through a pile of papers. She glanced up and her face broke into a smile as she saw Jessica. Within moments she had found a spare chair and fetched coffee from the small canteen just outside the swing doors, and the two girls settled down to talk.

'Well, what's all the mystery, then?' Jessica swung her long auburn pony-tail over her shoulder and looked at Hilary with green-flecked hazel eyes. 'Who *is* this new man, anyway? Must be someone pretty well-known to walk in and take over a documentary series just like that. And what sort of series is it?'

'It's a series on various kinds of social conditions,' Hilary said, not answering Jessica's first question. 'He'll tell you about it himself, but I can tell you who some of the other directors are.' She named a few, and Jessica's eyebrows went up. Those weren't the sort of people to be involved in a series on trivial matters, more

entertainment than serious investigation. It was a mark
of regard to be invited to join such company, and she
felt more curious than ever about the new producer.
Surely he must be a well-known name himself—but as
she opened her mouth to ask Hilary again, the other
girl forestalled her.

'Some of the subjects are things like industrial
diseases, and one's about homelessness. They're to be
an hour long, less time for commercials of course, and
where possible they're to include some drama, to get the
message home. The one you'll be doing is going to be
tied up with a book on the subject—a novel. You'll be
dramatising scenes from that.'

'Sounds fascinating.' Jessica took a sip of coffee. An
hour-long documentary, with dramatisation! Just the
kind of thing she'd been longing to get her teeth into.
Whoever this producer was, he must have seen some of
her work before—must have a very good idea of her
capabilities. He was giving her a big chance, and she
made up her mind that she was going to take it, with
both hands. 'But you still haven't told me what it's
about.'

'I can't. He wants to talk to you about it himself
first.' Hilary finished her own coffee. 'I'm to take you
along to his office at eleven.' She hesitated. 'I can tell
you, he's taken this place by storm—woken us all up!
Mercia TV isn't going to know what's hit it!'

'But who *is* he?' Jessica persisted. 'And where's he
been until now? With the B.B.C. or what?'

'No, with TV London. And he's been abroad on one
of those big nature assignments.' Hilary stopped as if
she'd already said to much, and got quickly to her feet.
'It's almost eleven. I'll take you along now. He'll tell
you everything you want to know.'

Slightly bewildered, Jessica followed the production
assistant's slim figure out of the office and along the
corridor. She still hadn't had an answer to her
question—just who was this new whirlwind of a

producer who had apparently dropped out of the sky and landed in Shrewsbury, in the offices of Mercia TV—but she would know in a few moments now. There was barely time, in fact, to wonder about Hilary's oddly evasive manner before they were stopping at one of the doors and answering the curt 'Come in' that followed Hilary's knock.

And then Hilary had slipped away with a peculiarly apologetic smile, and Jessica was entering alone—to look at the room's occupant with a puzzled curiosity that changed, almost in slow motion, through blank amazement and, as she took in every detail of the tall, dark-haried man who stood impassively before her, to a baffled anger and finally something very near panic.

'Matt!' she whispered through a throat that had suddenly gone dry, and instinctively she backed away towards the door. 'Don't run away, Jessica,' he said in the deep, powerful voice that had once sent excitement pulsing through her body. 'Come and sit down. We've got some talking to do.'

Dazed, Jessica moved slowly forward and sank into the low chair he had indicated, and Matt came round his desk to sit opposite her. His light grey eyes were still fixed on her with that disturbing intentness, and Jessica turned her head away. It had been too much of a shock—why hadn't Hilary *told* her, for God's sake? She must have known how she would feel.

'I asked Hilary especially not to warn you,' said Matt, divining her thoughts in the uncanny way he had always had. 'I didn't want to take any risks.'

Jessica found her voice, still dry and cracked but at least a decibel or so louder than her first stricken whisper. 'Risks?'

'Of your running away,' Matt said calmly. 'That was your first reaction, wasn't it? Fortunately, shock made it impossible—but if you'd known beforehand, you'd never have entered this room, would you? Not willingly, anyway.'

'No, I don't suppose I would.' The first wave of shock had begun to subside and Jessica met his eyes, firmly repressing any emotion that might be struggling to wake in her. 'And is that any wonder? I've managed to keep away from you for four years, Matt, and there's no reason why I should want to change anything now.'

'No?' He smiled infuriatingly. 'Well, we won't discuss that now. Let's talk about the film instead——'

'The *film*? You—mean—*you're* the producer?' As soon as the words were out Jessica cursed herself for her stupidity. *Obviously* he was the producer—it was just that seeing him so unexpectedly had driven all thoughts of the film from her head. She bit her lip and looked away again, unable to bear the look of amusement on Matt's face. God, what was happening to her? It had taken her four years to get this man out of her system—four years' pain, loneliness and struggle. Was she going to let him get to her now? More important, was she going to be able to work with him? And why had he asked for her as director—just what was he playing at?

Jessica watched suspiciously as Matt leaned back in his chair and lit a small cigar. So he hadn't given up that habit. . . . She shook herself mentally. Letting herself be reminded of the past wasn't going to help. If she and Matt were to work together—and just at present she doubted that very much indeed—she would be better advised to wipe her mind clear of everything that had happened before—act as if they'd only just met for the first time. Treat him as a stranger.

'Perhaps you could tell me something about the film,' she said politely, and saw Matt's eyes widen a little. That's a good start, she thought, and felt a touch of confidence creep through her. Yes, she could handle this all right. And at the end of the interview she would take great pleasure in refusing Matt's offer, however interesting it might be. There would be other films to direct. She had, after all, attained a position in which she could choose her work.

'All right,' said Matt, his voice cool. 'After all, there can't be anything else for us to discuss, can there? Not after four years. . . . You've done well in those four years, Jessica, incidentally. From production assistant to director—quite a dizzying climb. Done some good work too, I believe.'

'You haven't done so badly yourself,' Jessica said lightly. She'd no objection to bandying the odd compliment. . . . 'All those penetrating documentaries for TV London, not to mention *Nature Search*. What I find difficult to understand is why you should drop all that and come to a little regional station like Mercia TV. Won't it be all too parochial for you?'

Matt's eyes narrowed dangerously, but his tone was as light as Jessica's as he answered. "Oh, I don't think so. There's nothing more important than the grass roots, is there? That's what it's all about. And I haven't dropped my other interests. I have my own production company as well, you know, and I'm planning something quite big in association with one of the Australian networks. I shan't exactly disappear into the straw.'

'I'm sure all your fans will be relieved to hear it,' Jessica said sweetly, and caught a flash from the grey eyes. But again Matt suppressed the evident irritation she had aroused, and leant over to pick up some papers from his desk.

Jessica watched him through her long lashes. Four years had wrought a subtle change in him. It wasn't so much that he'd aged as strengthened—that was the only word she could find to describe the hard line of his jaw, the firmness of his finely-moulded lips, the cool determination of those light grey eyes. His body too was lean, without an ounce of spare flesh, taut in every muscular line, and there was a relaxed confidence in his control that hadn't been there four years earlier and made him even more formidable, as if he knew without a shadow of doubt that nothing could beat him. Or perhaps her observations were just an effect of their altered relationship, she mused. Her own body felt tense, alert for danger in this unexpected meeting. Was Matt, too, prepared for danger—even though he'd engineered it?

'I take it Hilary didn't tell you anything about this series?' Matt enquired, leafing through the papers. 'Apart from its being concerned with a variety of social conditions, anyway. Right—well, these conditions are all of local interest, things you'll find in the area covered by Mercia TV on both sides of the Welsh border. The diseases suffered by Welsh slateworkers— homelessness in remoter areas and towns like Shrewsbury itself, low pay in agriculture—that kind of thing. The particular subject I'd like you to tackle——' he flicked rapidly through the papers with long, sensitive fingers '—is that of the Welsh holiday cottage. You know—the small places that make such ideal second homes, bought up by people who just use them at weekends, depriving locals of homes. The problems are well-known and often end in tragedy—a lot of these cottages have been burned down by resentful Welsh extremists.' He glanced up, his needle-bright eyes meeting Jessica's before she could look away. 'Interest you?'

'Yes, it does,' she said slowly, already beginning to regret her decision to refuse the job, yet knowing that she could never work with Matt. If only it could have been another producer giving her this chance! 'How do you mean it to be tackled?'

'In the same style as the rest of the series. A mixture of straight documentary and drama, letting each complement the other and tell their own story. No narration or question-and-answer interviews. Just people talking, action and the drama scenes. It's a highly-effective technique, though it's more difficult to put together.'

'And the drama? Who does the script?' Jessica found herself unable to keep the note of eagerness out of her voice. It was so much the kind of thing she loved doing and knew she did well—creative and imaginative without losing sight of its serious documentary purpose. Already her mind was beginning to work, thinking, planning—abruptly, she reminded herself that she wasn't going to do it. She was going to refuse, if only for the pleasure of seeing Matt's face.

'Ah, now the drama for this particular film is especially interesting.' Matt slanted a grin at her and she was reminded with a shock of the quirky, almost leprechaun charm he could summon up on occasion. 'You're really in luck there, Jessica. You'll be using a novel by Emlyn Thomas. And not only will you be using his book, you'll be using the man himself. He's got quite a lot to say on the subject and he did a lot of research for the book.'

Jessica stared at him. Emlyn Thomas—one of the foremost writers of the day, runner-up for the Booker Prize, known as the most passionate Welsh writer since his unrelated namesake Dylan, yet combining fervour with balance and insight. She was to use *him*—and his novel—in her programme? A bubble of excitement welled up in her—and then she caught Matt's bright, sardonic glance and remembered her vow.

Not even for a chance like that could she work with Matt. It was out—right out. It had to be. It had taken her four years to overcome Matt's devastating effect on her, and she couldn't risk going through that again. Once again she wished that Hilary had told her, given her some hint. If she'd known that Matt was in this room, in this building, she'd have turned tail and just not stopped running.

'So let's get down to work,' Matt was saying easily. 'It's a fifty-five-minute programme, Jessica, and that's a lot of minutes to fill. I want it as tight as possible too, but you'll need quite a bit of atmosphere. You'll have to find locations, too. Chris Kirk will be researching for you, and he's——'

Almost desperately, Jessica interrupted him. She couldn't let this go on any longer—this assumption that she was going to work with him as if nothing had ever happened. And she didn't even want to think about the film—the film that, in any other circumstances, she'd have given her ears to make.

'I'm sorry, Matt,' she said, trying to keep the tremor out of her voice, 'you're wasting your time. It sounds a marvellous film, and I'm sure it will be. But you'll have to find some other director, because I won't be making it.'

Matt stopped abruptly and shot her a glance that seemed to sear straight into her mind. Jessica's hazel eyes dropped and she fluttered her long lashes over them, shaken by the inimical quality of his look. Her long hair lay like a flame over her shoulder and she twined her fingers in it, wishing that she had the courage to get up and walk out of the room. But one glance at Matt's taut body told her that it would be no use trying. All the alertness of a jungle cat was implicit in those lean muscles, and if she so much as moved towards the door he would be there first—and then God only knew what would happen! Jessica repressed a shiver and stared down at her fingers.

'Won't be making it?' Matt repeated, his voice like steel wire. 'And why not, may I ask? You've no other commitments—I checked.'

'Maybe not.' Try as she might, there was still a faint, betraying shake in her voice. 'But I *am* freelance, Matt. I do have the right to say yes or no if I choose. And this time I choose to say no.'

Matt stared at her. Heavy, dark brows came down over his steely eyes, and Jessica tried not to remember that those eyes could at times be as soft as pigeons' wings. The lines of his face were harsh and uncompromising, making him look suddenly more than his ten years older than her. He had always been ruthless in anger, she recalled, and shivered again.

'You—choose—to say—no,' he repeated disbelievingly. 'Jessica, you're out of your mind! This series is going to be important. Every programme will be shown nationally—not just on Mercia, with the faint possibility of appearing on some other region when they happen to have a gap. There'll be previews—it will be selected for prime viewing, not just by the daily papers but by the Sundays as well. And afterwards there'll be reviews. It's the best chance you've ever had, Jessica—my God, the names of the other directors should have told you that! You can't *afford* to say no!'

Jessica raised her eyes and met his obstinately. All that he said was true—she knew it all too well. But she *wasn't* going to work with him. It was impossible—the whole idea. She was amazed that he'd ever thought it could work.

'You're letting your emotions rule you again,' Matt accused her, uncoiling himself from his chair to stride up and down the office. 'Obviously you *still* haven't grown up, even after four years. You're—what is it? Twenty-eight?—yet you're still behaving like a spoilt adolescent. Sulking because someone didn't behave just how you wanted them to, taking every little slight as a mortal wound, playing the game of if-you-won't-let-me-bowl-I'll-take-my-bat-home—my God, how childish can you get? This is *work*, Jessica—I'm offering you a chance, a big chance. Or perhaps you'd rather I decided to be childish too, and gave it to someone else, just out of spite?'

'I'd rather you offered it to someone else, full stop,' she flashed back. 'I've told you, Matt, I don't want to do it. My reasons are my own affair——'

'Oh no, they're not,' he retorted grimly. 'Not when they concern me, anyway. And those reasons—if we're to dignify them with the name—most definitely *do* concern me. *Don't they?*'

Jessica's gasp was almost a small scream as Matt came to a halt before her and bent over, his hands gripping her shoulders fiercely. She felt the tensile strength in them and twisted frantically under his grasp, but although his fingers loosened fractionally from their first cruel bite, there was no getting away from them. Imploringly, she looked up into the face that was so near hers, and felt an involuntary twist of the stomach as his breath touched her cheek. They'd been close like this so often—the memory was a pain far crueller than his hands could ever be.

Matt's expression changed as their eyes met and he jerked away from her, turning so that she couldn't see his face. His back was rigid and Jessica shrank in her chair, almost afraid to move unless she provoked another outburst of violence. Surreptitiously, she touched her shoulders, wincing at the tenderness his fingers had left there. He'd always been a bully, she told herself. Always thought that brute force was the way to win an argument.

'Well?' Matt asked after a moment, and his voice was now tightly controlled. 'Don't they concern me—those reasons of yours for refusing what must be the biggest plum to drop in your lap in your whole career to date? Isn't it just that you don't want to work with me—that you're *afraid* to work with me?'

His voice had a sneer in it that cut right through Jessica's panic and brought her upright in her chair. Afraid! Yes, she was, of course she was—but did she have to give Matt the satisfaction of knowing it? And it certainly would be a satisfaction, she thought bitterly, staring up into his mocking face as he swung round on her. He might be telling himself he wanted her to take this job, but he'd be far more pleased if she didn't, through fear of him.

'I'm not in the least afraid of you,' she said, putting as much ice as she knew how into her voice. 'Why on earth should I be? Except for the fact that you're physically stronger, of course. But you'd hardly be likely to use force on the set. There would be too many people about to see, wouldn't there?'

It gave her some satisfaction of her own to see him flinch at the implication that any bullying would be done in private. Mentally, she scored a round to herself. But that didn't mean she would be likely to win the whole game. She wasn't even going to play it.

'So why are you refusing?' Matt persisted inexorably. 'I want a good reason, Jessica.'

'And I've told you, I don't have to give any reason at all,' she retorted. 'Just that I don't want to do it. All right, the idea of working with you doesn't exactly thrill me—and I can't really believe it thrills you, either. Why don't *you* answer a few questions, Matt? Like just why you're so keen for me to take this on—and why you came to Mercia TV at all?'

Matt ran a hand through his thick dark hair, giving a sigh of exasperation as he did so. 'What in hell's name has that got to do with it?' he expostulated. 'I've already told you anyway, why I'm here. I like the idea of doing some regional TV, and I like this region. Shropshire, the Welsh Marches, Wales itself—there's an atmosphere about it all, a character you don't find anywhere else. All right, maybe you think I should have kept away, knowing that you were here—but life can't be arranged like that, Jessica. We're not territorial animals with our own boundaries marked out that others mustn't cross. Even so, I thought long and hard before coming—and it may please you to know that I was grateful for the chance of offering you this particular programme to do. Call it an olive branch if you like—I just knew that it was something you could do and do well, and I wouldn't have been doing my own job properly if I hadn't offered it to you. And on top of that, I thought it might indicate to you that I was prepared for us to work together, whatever happened in the past.'

Jessica stared at him doubtfully. It sounded almost true—or was it just that little bit too facile? Knowing Matt, she was sure there was some other reason—some reason he hadn't told her and didn't intend to. And that reason would be the most important; the one most dangerous to her.

'Look,' said Matt, his voice once again velvety with persuasion, 'why don't we start again from square one? I'm offering you the chance to make a film you can really go to town on—a film that'll be seen all over the country and taken seriously by everyone. You know you'd jump at the chance normally. It's only because I'm producing it that you've refused. Can't you forget that? Treat me as a producer like any other, someone you don't know privately at all, someone you perhaps don't like very much but can still work with *because it's your job*. Can't you bring your professionalism to your aid? Isn't that something we all have to do?'

Jessica clasped her hands in front of her face, elbows on knees, pinching her lips between her thumbs. She was caught, she knew. Matt had attacked her on two fronts—playing on her fear of him, knowing that she would never admit it, and now on her professional pride. Try as she might, there was no acceptable reason she could think up for refusing to do the film. And she *wanted* to do it, that was the most galling part. He'd known her well enough—still knew her well enough, after all this time—to see that this was just her kind of documentary. And he must be sure that she'd make a good job of it. By choosing her at all, he was putting his own reputation on the line.

'Well?' Matt said again, his voice soft. 'Look, Jessica, if it helps at all I shan't even be here for a lot of the time. I'm booked to go to Africa soon on an anthropological assignment. You'll be working with my assistant producer more than you will with me.'

Jessica looked up quickly. An *assistant* producer! She might not even have to have any contact with Matt at all. Why hadn't he said so before—it could have saved all this trouble. But that wouldn't have been his way, would it? No, he'd have enjoyed watching her squirm, taken pleasure in her indecision. He'd always like displaying his power over her.

'Does that make a difference?' Matt was watching her closely. 'Well, unflattering though it may be, I'll accept that it does. So can I take it that *you'll* accept the job?'

Jessica nodded reluctantly. If there'd been any way of accepting without letting Matt savour his triumph, she would have taken it, but there was none. All the same, she didn't have to let him gloat too much. He might have won, but the power he had once had over her no longer existed, and the sooner she could make him see that the better it would be. She would make this film—and she would do her very best with it, because Matt's words about the opportunity it offered to her own career were all quite true. But once it was over, she would be looking for another company to work with. If Matt had joined Mercia TV, it was time for Jessica to leave. There was no way she could continue to work with him—no way at all.

'That's settled, then?' Matt was still watching her. 'You won't go back on it? I can't afford any chopping or changing, Jessica.'

'I won't go back on it,' she answered steadily. 'You know very well it's just the kind of thing I want to do. So long as we don't have any more contact than we absolutely have to, Matt. I'm not going to pretend I'm overcome with joy to see you again.'

'Oh, you've left me in no doubt about that,' he said dryly. 'Though there are certainly things we have to discuss—about ourselves as well as about the film. So I'm afraid you'll have to see me some time, Jessica. Perhaps for dinner one evening? The atmosphere might be a little more conducive to private conversation than this rather stark office.'

'I'm sorry you think it's stark,' Jessica said coolly.

'Obviously you've been accustomed to much more opulence at TV London. And no, I don't think we'll have dinner, Matt. There really isn't any private conversation that I can think of that we could enjoy. And I don't think we have anything to discuss about ourselves.'

Her heart jinked suddenly as Matt moved closer, leaning over and resting his hands on the back of her chair, one each side of her. Jessica stared up at him, trying desperately to stay cool, to prevent him from sensing the wild beating of her pulses, the quickening of her breath. She cursed herself silently—surely after four years she should be able to resist the physical attraction that he had always had for her. Hadn't that been her downfall in the past—hadn't it been that purely physical magnetism that had drawn her to him as a candle draws a moth, and kept her fluttering about him even when she had known he could never be any good to her?

Hadn't it been that purely physical desire that had made her marry him?

With an almost convulsive movement she jerked to her feet, thrusting Matt aside. She couldn't sit there a moment longer, watching him come nearer, feeling his closeness, experiencing again the unique male scent of his body unadulterated by any artificial aid. In another moment he would have kissed her, she was sure; and she just couldn't afford to let that happen. Not if she were to retain any self-respect at all.

Matt was upright again, watching her narrowly as she made for the door. When she reached it, she turned and faced him, panting slightly and trembling with a mixture of panic and triumph. But the look on his face turned her cold. She hadn't won at all. Her sudden flight had told him all he wanted to know—that she was still highly susceptible to him. And the quiet satisfaction of his expression indicated, as clearly as if he had said so out loud, that that was enough. He knew now just how vulnerable she was—and Jessica was all too well aware that he wouldn't hesitate to use that knowledge.

She went through the door, closed it and leant back against it, shaking uncontrollably. What had she done, accepting that assignment against all her instincts? How could she have given her word, promised not to go back on it? Matt—Matt Fenwood, the man she had married six years ago and parted from after only two years— was now in a position she had sworn she would never let him occupy again. A position of power over her. And this time she couldn't run away.

CHAPTER TWO

'WELL—here's to the film.' Chris Kirk raised his glass and Jessica did the same, smiling. It was one of the compensations of this assignment that Christ was her researcher. They had known each other for several years now and worked together before, becoming firm friends. Just at present there was a particular closeness between them.

'This was a good idea,' she said, glancing round the dimly-lit little restaurant with its oak beams and warm red carpet. 'I always like coming here, and it's nice to have a chance to discuss things away from the office.'

'Well, one is a little less prone to interruption,' Chris grinned. 'Though of course I did have an ulterior motive. I've been looking for an excuse to ask you out for weeks!'

Jessica glanced at him, a trifle disturbed by something in his voice. He'd sounded almost serious— and although a smile still stayed on his lips, his eyes were sombre. She looked away again quickly. One of the main advantages of Chris's company had always been that he never made any emotional demands on her. If that were to change—well, all she knew was that she didn't want it to. Life was quite complicated enough already.

At that moment their food arrived and the awkward moment passed. For a few minutes they concentrated on the meal in front of them, and when Chris spoke again that slight edge of intensity in his voice had gone and he was his normal cheerful self.

'It's an interesting subject, isn't it? The film, I mean. Of course, I know the news and current affairs programmes have dealt with the problem, but nobody's made a full-length documentary. Not like this, anyway.'

'No. And I like the idea of the drama. Have you read Emlyn Thomas's book?'

'*A Cottage in Wales*? Mm—powerful stuff.' Chris sliced his roast beef. 'What I like about it is that it shows both sides of the story. The hard-up farmer, naturally taking the best price he can get for his cottage and knowing that the kind of money the businessman's prepared to pay will solve his worries for life. The young couple who find themselves gazumped, with nowhere to live, forced to move to the city, resentful and unhappy—the wife in particular, losing the baby they're expecting and the husband blaming it on the area they live in and, from that, inevitably the businessman too. And then——'

'Setting fire to the cottage,' Jessica interrupted eagerly, 'knowing that thousands of pounds have been spent to make it a luxury home, even though it's only used for odd weekends. And finally the discovery that the businessman's wife is suffering from an incurable and progressive disease and just lives for the occasions when they can come to the place he's fitted up specially for her.... It's got it all, Chris, and with Emlyn Thomas's beautiful treatment there's no mawkishness or sentimentality. Everyone's got a point of view. The businessman, Robert Mercer, *isn't* the ruthless tycoon that young Huw and Olwen think him. Huw *isn't* the thug he might appear to be, just a young man driven to a frenzy of despair over what's happening. And even the farmer isn't the hard-hearted, mercenary grasper he could be—just a struggling hill-farmer with a lot of rather unproductive land and a heavy tax burden to cope with. Naturally he accepts a high price when it's offered! Mercer doesn't realise he's gazumping the younger couple and they don't know about his wife. They're all just trying to live the best way they can, not even aware of the devastation they're causing in each other's lives. And these things *happen*, Chris. They're happening all the time.'

'And that's what's going to make it a good documentary. Chris hesitated for a moment. 'I'm glad you've taken it on, Jessica. You'll make a fine job of it. I must admit I was a bit worried—when I heard that Matt was producing.'

'Yes . . . well. . . .' The light of enthusiasm died out of Jessica's face. 'I nearly didn't, Chris. The thought of working with Matt again. . . . And I didn't even *know*. Not until I walked into his office. He'd made Hilary promise not to warn me—though I still think she could have given me a hint.'

'That must have been one hell of a shock,' Chris said sympathetically, and Jessica nodded.

'It was. And he knew it too. I think he even enjoyed it—the bastard!' She bit her lip, aware of the venom in her voice, and went on more quietly, 'It put me in a rotten position, Chris. I knew I could do the job and I wanted to. But I just couldn't see any way Matt and I could work together. All right, perhaps that's not very adult. But it's how I felt.'

'I can understand it.' Chris's voice was warm. 'Even after—how long is it since you split up?'

'Over four years now.' Jessica finished her trout and laid her knife and fork on the plate. 'Twice as long as we were married! But—well, I'd hoped I'd got over it. I haven't really thought about him for ages. Work's taken up a lot of my time and I just tried to put all that out of my head. And then, seeing him again like that, with no warning—well. . . .'

'It all came surging back,' Chris said quietly. 'The hurt, the misery, everything.'

'Yes, that's just how it was. But how did you——' Jessica met his eyes, then looked away quickly. 'I'm sorry, Chris. I'd forgotten about you and Sue. No wonder you understand so well.'

Chris shrugged. 'I guess it's something we all ought

to understand—it seems to happen to so many people. But I must admit that I thought you and Matt would make it—though I didn't know you all that well then.'

Jessica shook her head. 'Matt and I should never have married. We're like fire and water—we just couldn't mix. Oh, the physical attraction was there all right—that's what fooled us. We took it for love. But it isn't, is it? It's just a part of love, and if the rest is missing it just isn't strong enough.'

Chris contemplated for a moment while the waiter took away their plates. Then he said thoughtfully, 'I wouldn't have said you were fire and water, Jessica. Fire and fire, perhaps. In some ways you're very alike, you and Matt. Maybe that was the trouble—you struck sparks off each other.'

Jessica stared at him, shaken by his insight. That was just what she and Matt had done—struck sparks of each other. Their marriage had been a continual series of electric storms, and the lightning had eventually burnt them up. Or so she'd thought. But it couldn't quite have done so—or why should she have known that fiercely pulsing current again yesterday, when she'd met Matt again?

Anxious suddenly to get off the subject, she looked at Chris and said, 'Was that what happened between you and Sue? I always thought *you* were entirely compatible.'

'Oh, me and Sue,' said Chris with a grimace. 'No, it was nothing so dramatic as that. Sue just got sick of being a TV researcher's wife. I don't blame her really. It wasn't much fun for her, stuck down there in Herefordshire by herself while I'm up here in Shrewsbury—especially once Jasper had come along. She was really tied then. It's not as if I can get home every evening—I can't, when we're on location or I'm working late.'

'Why didn't you move up here, then?' asked Jessica, and Chris shrugged.

'She wouldn't. Oh, I know it sounds as if she wanted
to eat her cake and have it—but I had to see her point
of view. If she did come up here she wouldn't see that
much more of me, and when I'm away—like that
American trip when we were off for two months—she'd
be entirely on her own. At least where we are now—
where she is, I mean—she's got her family around her,
she knows everyone in the village. As Sue herself said,
moving would just give her the privilege of cooking my
breakfast and not much more.'

Jessica was silent. She knew that this situation was a
common problem among TV staff, who often worked
long and unpredictable hours and became absorbed in
their work so that they barely noticed the reactions of
their families. It was difficult to know what the solution
was—if there even was a solution—and she felt helpless
to offer Chris any comfort. She wasn't even sure that he
needed it—he seemed to have come to terms with his
position—but his insight into her own feelings told her
that he'd suffered on his own account, and she wished
she could repay his understanding.

Chris didn't seem to mind her silence—perhaps it was
what he needed. After a moment, when they had chosen
their desserts and ordered coffee, he went back to
talking about the film.

'What's your first plan, Jessica? Any ideas as to
format and so on? Where do we start?'

'Well, I need as much information as possible about
cottages that have been sold away from the locals—the
kind of people who've bought them, what they're used
for, how often they're occupied. And of course we'll
need local reactions to them. Do the incomers take any
part in village life, do they ever become part of the
community—do they want to, or are they shut out? All
that's important. And cottages that have been burnt—
everything we can get on them. We'll need to film some
of them too. But I think my first move will be to visit
Emlyn Thomas and talk to him. He lives somewhere

near Snowdonia, doesn't he? I think he has to be my starting-point—I've got to get the dramatisation sorted out, find actors and locations, all that, before I can really decide on anything else.'

'Mm. Any idea what scenes you want to dramatise?'

'Well, I've only read the book through once, rather quickly. But I thought the one where the young couple, Huw and Olwen, discover they've been gazumped; probably I'd need to show the Mercers actually seeing it, that would come first. Then Huw and Olwen in the city, finding a squalid little flat, Huw looking for work, Olwen losing the baby; Huw setting fire to the cottage, of course, and then the Mercers seeing the damage. Something along those lines, anyway.'

Chris whistled softly. 'That's all going to be pretty expensive, Jessica. Especially if you want to do the fire scene. It'd have to be done at night—you'd need services standing by, fire engines and so on. *And* you've got to find a cottage to burn. All right for a major serial, but for this. . . .' His words trailed away into doubt.

'This *is* a major series,' Jessica said stubbornly. 'Matt made that very clear to me. It's going to be shown nationwide and it's going to be important. We've got to pull out all the stops on this, Chris. And that fire scene's essential. It's the core of the book and the core of the whole controversy.'

Chris said no more and they glanced up as the waiter arrived with their desserts. After that, they made a few preliminary arrangements and Chris agreed to start collecting information on the documentary aspects while Jessica worked on the drama. Both of them would go to see Emlyn Thomas as soon as it could be arranged.

It had been a pleasant and satisfying evening, Jessica thought later as she waved goodbye to Chris and let herself into her cottage in a small village near the town. She and Chris got along well both workwise and socially. An evening spent with him never failed to leave her feeling warmed by his friendship.

So why did the thought of Matt have to invade her mind at just that moment, making her change her plan to invite Chris in for a last drink? Why did the vision of her estranged husband come between them, preventing her from returning Chris's goodnight kiss with the warmth she wanted to, touching her voice with coolness as she thanked him for the meal?

Jessica went into the cottage and slammed the door as though she were trying to shut Matt out. As indeed she was, she acknowledged as she went into the kitchen and banged a saucepan down on the stove. But why did she have to, after all this time? Hadn't she wasted enough of her life on that man?

If Matt had deliberately tried to upset her life, he couldn't have done so any more effectively than by joining Mercia TV.

When Jessica climbed into bed half an hour later she was tired and ready for sleep. But sleep, it seemed, wasn't ready for her; as soon as the light went out she found herself staring into darkness, her overwrought brain seething with unwelcome memories, circling in an endless and pointless dance of torment through her restless mind.

The most persistent of these memories took her back over seven years, to the time when she had first met Matt Fenwood. She had just landed her first job as a production assistant with the B.B.C., after three years as a secretary, and was eager to do her best, determined to prove her worth. As a production assistant her duties were widely varied and liable to change at any moment, according to the requirements of the team. She could be arranging locations, typing schedules, timing rehearsals, checking continuity, making coffee and calming interviewees, all in the same morning. If anything went wrong, it was the production assistant's job to get it put right, and quickly. A good production assistant was worth her weight in gold; an inefficient one could very nearly wreck the whole enterprise. Jessica had been determined from the beginning to be a good one.

And so she had been. But her confidence had been shaken when she learned that her first solo job was to be with one of the great Matt Fenwood's documentaries.

'Couldn't they have picked anyone else?' she'd asked, staring in panic at Maggy Payne, who had guided her through the maze so far. 'I mean, this is my first job on my own—I'll make all kinds of stupid mistakes. And Matt Fenwood isn't famous for suffering fools gladly.'

'Which needn't worry you in the slightest, since you're not a fool,' Maggy replied calmly. 'Look, Jess, we've worked together long enough now for me to know what you're capable of—and you can do as well as me. You've coped with all the situations we've come up against without turning a hair, and there's no reason why you should change. You've got enough initiative to deal with anything unexpected and even Matt Fenwood doesn't expect miracles. Stop worrying and go out there and enjoy it.' She smiled dreamily. 'He's not just a slavedriver, you know. There's another side to him, too.'

Jessica glanced at her sharply. 'Yes, I've heard about that as well,' she answered shortly. 'And I don't want to become his latest conquest, either. I might admire him more if he was a bit choosier—but Matt Fenwood has so many girl-friends it's not even a compliment!'

'Oh, that's nonsense. Look at the girl-friends he has—they're something special, every one of them, you have to admit that. Top actresses—society girls—models—newsreaders. I would have thought it was very much a compliment to be noticed by Matt.'

'I'm amazed you didn't angle for the job, then,' Jessica remarked a little acidly, and Maggy laughed.

'Oh, there wouldn't be a chance. He's never been

known to look as low as a mere P.A. No, you go along and admire from a distance, Jess. You'll be safe enough, and you'll learn a lot from his direction, if that's where your ambitions lie.'

Jessica felt a spark of interest. She was indeed keen to become a director one day, and she had already picked up quite a few points from the films she'd worked on with Maggy. To work with someone like Matt Fenwood really was a chance to learn a lot. If only she didn't do something idiotic. . . .

'Look, you'll be fine,' Maggy reassured her. 'He's not a monster and he knows this is your first real job. Don't worry about it.'

And Jessica had discovered the truth of Maggy's words on her very first day, when Matt had taken advantage of a lull in the discussions to come across to her.

'Hello, Jessica. I don't think we've met before, have we?' His grey eyes assessed her, but in a friendly manner. 'Well, Maggy's told me about you and I understand you've worked with her quite a bit. So I think we'll get along all right. Just keep on your toes and don't burst into tears if I shout at you in a fraught moment.' He grinned, showing white teeth, and Jessica felt a sudden warmth relaxing her taut nerves. 'I won't even apologise afterwards—it's all part of the job, and no ill-feelings, okay?'

'Okay, Mr Fenwood,' Jessica smiled, and he closed his eyes in a parody of pain.

'*Mr Fenwood?* Haven't you been working here long enough to know that it's Christian names all round?' He laid his hand on her shoulder and drew her a little closer, and Jessica was conscious of a quickening of her heartbeat. 'Matt, right? And now let's make sure you know everyone else.'

Still keeping his arm lightly across her shoulders, he led her round the room, introducing her to the rest of the crew; cameramen, sound recordists, location assistant and floor manager. Some of them Jessica already knew, but she was glad of the chance to meet the others. Usually it was simply a case of getting to know each other as they went along.

After that, Matt Fenwood could do no wrong in her eyes. To her anxiety to do the job well for its own sake, she added the need to do it well for his, and she was constantly at his elbow, ready to interpret and carry out his slightest wish and ensure that she did everything in her power to make the production run smoothly. And because she was so keen, and Matt was acknowledged to be a brilliant director, getting the best out of every crew he worked with, the production did run smoothly, and the film was acclaimed by TV critics and shown on all the networks.

It was only after it was all over and Jessica was back in the office doing the humdrum tasks that inevitably followed a production that she realised just what had happened.

There hadn't been time for introspection before this. Once a production had started, everyone worked flat out, and the days were filled with filming, both in studios and on location, returning only for a meal and a night's sleep before starting again the next day. Occasionally there would be time to see the rushes of filming already taken, and Jessica was invariably busy in what there was left of her evenings in planning what she needed to do next day. There was no time to think about anything else, and any time there was seemed better spent in sleeping. Sleep became a top priority during those days and weeks.

But once they were over and life returned to normal, there was time to think again. And as Jessica worked at her desk, doing a job that needed only half her mind, she found herself thinking about Matt.

She thought about him as she walked back from work to the tiny flat she had found half a mile away from the studios. She thought about him in the morning when she woke up. She lay awake thinking about him, going over all the things he'd said and done, the way he'd looked at her with those glinting grey eyes. And the only reason she'd allowed herself to go to sleep at all was because she hoped she might dream about him.

I'm in love with him, she thought incredulously. In love with Matt Fenwood. Oh, Matt ... Matt. ...

There wasn't a chance, of course. Everyone knew that Matt was seeing Elaine Kelly, and in any case, as Maggy had said, he'd never look at a mere P.A. But a girl could dream, couldn't she ...?

Jessica lost weight over the next few weeks and her previously slightly plump figure became instead a slender, softly curved shape. Her long hair shone like a chestnut from much brushing and she was careful always to look her best when she went to work. There was always the chance of meeting Matt there. Always the chance that he might—just might—this time look at a mere production assistant. ...

And so he did. But it wasn't when Jessica was looking her best; and afterwards, thinking it over, she was astonished that he'd looked at her at all.

It had been raining hard that morning when she left for work. For once, she was late; as she'd hurried to get dressed, the zip on her skirt had broken and she'd had to wear jeans, her other skirt being still damp from the wash. That meant an entire change from tights and slip, and a frenzied search for a sweater. Coming out of the flat she kicked over a bottle of milk, which spread a white flood down the steps, and she had to fetch a dustpan and brush to sweep up the broken glass; the milk she left for the neighbours' cat, hoping that it wouldn't cut its tongue on any glass she'd overlooked.

By this time the rain was beating against her in the strong wind. Jessica set off to walk to the studios, turning her collar up round her neck because she'd forgotten her umbrella in the panic. But she had nothing to cover her head with, and her hair had turned a dark red by the time Matt drew up beside her in his car.

'Want a lift?'

Startled, Jessica whipped round, her delight at seeing him immediately sinking as she realised what she must look like.

'Oh, Matt!—yes, please, I'd love one.' She scrambled in beside him and he clipped the safety-belt round her, his arms lightly round her as he did so. Jessica sat very still, hoping that he couldn't feel the sudden wild beating of her heart.

'Haven't seen you for some time,' he remarked as he drove off again. 'Been busy?'

'Yes.' Jessica told him about the production she'd worked on since his film and he nodded, keeping his eyes on the road.

'Sounds interesting. I've been abroad—Spain. Only got back yesterday. Maybe we'll be able to work together again soon. How would you like that?'

His tone was light and casual, but he took his eyes off the traffic to look at her and Jessica was startled by the intentness of his smoky eyes.

'I—I'd like it very much.'

'Have to see what we can arrange,' he murmured, and turned into the car park. 'Well, there we are, little drowned rat. I expect you want to dash in and tidy up. Be seeing you!'

Jessica slipped out of the car, too mortified to look at him or do more than mutter a hasty thank-you. She ran through the driving rain into the building and made straight for the cloakroom. *Drowned rat!* That's what he'd called her! And as she stared into the mirror and rubbed ineffectively at her soaked hair with a handkerchief, she had to admit that the description fitted. But did he have to make it quite so plain that he wasn't prepared to be seen walking through the doors in her company?

Well, he wouldn't be asking for *her* as his P.A. again,

that was certain! Whatever he'd said, it was obviously nothing more than empty politeness. Jessica would be very surprised if she ever heard any more from him.

But in that, she was wrong. She heard from him that very afternoon. And by that time, her hair dried and brushed out to a shimmering copper cloud on her shoulders, it was clear that he didn't see her any more as a drowned rat.

'Hi, Jessica. Recovered from your swim?' There was a glint of laughter in his eyes, but it wasn't mocking laughter and Jessica smiled back. 'Look, I've got a proposition to put to you,' he went on, dropping into a spare chair by Jessica's desk. 'I'm just about to start work on a new documentary. It means a lot of work and I want a couple of reliable P.A.s. Maggy's free and I see you are too. How about it?'

Jessica stared at him. He was *asking* her to be his P.A. again! And if he needed two, it must be quite a large production. She opened her mouth to ask questions but he spoke again.

'It means going away for several weeks—to California. Are you interested, Jessica?'

'*Interested?*' she got out. 'You must be joking! Of course I'm interested!'

'That's fine, then. I'll let you have all the details in the next day or two. We'll be flying to San Francisco and going up into the Yosemite National Park. I'm doing a film about gold-prospectors—modern ones—and there are quite a few up there, panning away at their claims. Should be quite interesting.'

'Yes,' Jessica said faintly, still unable to believe her ears, 'it should be.'

'So look out your passport and see about getting a visa, all right? I'll be calling a conference soon—we won't actually be going for a couple of months, but as you know there'll be a lot to get done before then. Okay?' Once again he gave her that disturbingly intent look, and then he was gone, leaving Jessica stunned and shaking at her desk.

A trip to California, with Matt Fenwood! If nothing else came of it, she'd have an experience to remember all her life. But was it, after all, so certain that nothing would come of it? Jessica remembered that intent look and shivered.

It had indeed been a trip to remember, she thought now, tossing uncomfortably in a bed that seemed tonight to be filled with rocks. In every way. It had been the beginning of a period of intense happiness. But when she recalled the depths of the anguish that had followed, she wondered if it had been worth it. If she had never been so happy, she would never have been so miserable either; and the misery had lasted longer. Twice as long.

She thumped the pillow, trying to find a comfortable spot for her head. It did no good to go over these old memories. Better to forget them, think instead of the productions she was concerned with now, her own film about Welsh cottages. But Matt was involved in that too, and before she could prevent them her thoughts had slipped back to that visit to California over six years earlier.

It had been Jessica's first visit to America and she had been like a wide-eyed child, taking in everything, noting all the differences large and small, feeling rather as if she were taking part in a film herself. They spent a day in San Francisco to recover from jet-lag, but few of the crew took advantage of the time to rest and they wandered in a group along Fisherman's Wharf, rode on the cable-cars, and ended up in Chinatown, sharing a huge pot of fragrant weak tea and eating the best Chinese meal Jessica had ever had. And all the time, Matt had been there; walking by her side, sitting across the table from her, keeping her safe on the side of the rattling cable-car with a strong arm held firmly across her shoulders.

And then there had been the days spent up in the

mountains, following the rushing rivers as they carried
melt-water down from the snows, bringing gold-bearing
debris to the waiting prospectors. Some of them did use
the old panning method, but these, Jessica discovered,
were mostly locals who did it for a hobby, or people out
from the city on weekends. More serious prospectors
used an appliance like a large vacuum cleaner to suck
the debris from the riverbed and pass it through a sluice
where it could be filtered. It all made picturesque
filming along the wild banks, with the rugged *sierras*
towering above.

On their last evening, Matt and Jessica wandered by
themselves out of the motel, close to the gate of the
Yosemite National Park, and strolled together through
a gathering dusk by the river. It was a foaming,
turbulent river, the water sliding like green ice over the
smooth brown rocks to shatter like glass beneath,
sending a thousand splintering drops shimmering into
the air. High above, in the dark blue sky, Jessica could
see the wheeling shape of a turkey vulture still looking
for a last meal; smaller birds hopped about the rocks,
flying a few yards as she and Matt approached,
watching with beady eyes and then returning as they
passed.

Matt found a moss-covered boulder and sat down,
drawing her down beside him. He kept his arm around
her and they sat without speaking, watching the torrent
and listening to its music.

'It's been a good shoot,' Matt said at last, his lips
close to Jessica's hair. 'And no small credit to you.
You've done well, Jessica.'

Jessica made a small sound. She didn't want to talk
about the shoot; nobody had talked about anything
else, it seemed, for weeks. Just for this last evening, she
wanted to pretend it was just her and Matt here
together; that none of the others, back in the motel,
existed.

'Good place for a holiday, this,' Matt observed after

a few moments. 'I should think it's pretty busy in the season. This'd be the best time to come—when the snows are melting and the people haven't arrived yet. Spring—it's usually the best time anywhere.'

'For a holiday?' Jessica murmured, letting her head rest on his shoulder.

'For a special sort of holiday, yes. A holiday that means a new start.' And as Jessica turned her head to look at him enquiringly, he added with that strange, intent look that twisted her heart: 'For a honeymoon.'

'A—a honeymoon?' Jessica's heart was beating so hard that it seemed to choke her words. 'I—I didn't know you were thinking of getting married.'

'Neither did I—until we came here.' Matt pulled her closer and his free hand came up and stroked her smooth, coppery hair. 'What about it, Jessica? Would you like a honeymoon with me? Damn it——' his voice roughened '—what I'm saying, girl, is will you marry me? As soon as possible—I'm not accustomed to waiting for what I want!'

There was a moment's perfect silence; even the water seemed to pause as Jessica stared at Matt and tried to assimilate his words. *Marry* him? Marry Matt Fenwood? Was she out of her mind, or was this some kind of dream—the kind of dream she'd hoped for those nights when she'd been reluctant to go to sleep because she'd have to stop thinking about him?

'Don't look at me like that, Jessica,' he said softly in that deep velvety voice of his. 'Or have I grown two heads without realising it?'

Wordlessly, Jessica shook her head, and he smiled and drew her head close to his. 'Maybe this will help you to make up your mind,' he murmured, and laid his lips on hers.

After the first tiny gasp of shock, Jessica found herself responding almost involuntarily to Matt's kiss. Her lips quivered against his, parting under his gentle yet inexorable pressure; and as she felt his hands slip

caressingly down her body to gather her closer against
him, a tremor ran through her and her own hands
found his body and gripped him tightly, fingers moving
in the roughness of his sweater.

The kiss was longer and deeper than any Jessica had
known; the few boy-friends she'd had previously had
been on a much more casual basis, and if they had
shown signs of wanting to become more serious
something had made her back off. She had even, once
or twice, began to wonder if she had a naturally cold
disposition. But any fears on that score were certainly
dispelled now, as she clung to Matt, returning his kiss
with her own half-shy exploration, letting her fingers
find their way into his thick, dark hair, moving in his
arms to press her body closer to his, and whimpering
with delight as she felt the strong beat of his heart
against her own.

'Can I take it that the answer is yes?' he breathed at
last, taking his lips from hers but keeping them
tantalisingly close.

'The answer . . .?' In the whirl of breathtaking
emotion, Jessica had almost forgotten that he had just
asked her to marry him. 'But I didn't know—I had no
idea——'

'This is all so sudden, in fact!' he mocked her gently.
'My dear girl, didn't you realise I was interested in you?
Haven't I spent most of these past few weeks with
you—walking with you, talking with you, sitting with
you? Didn't that mean *anything*?'

'But that was work,' said Jessica, turning to stare
bemused at the white-flecked river.

'Work? It was pleasure, sheer pleasure. I don't always
rely on my P.A. to that extent, I may tell you—I
generally like to give the poor girl at least a few hours
to herself. But you—Jessica, you've been like a breath
of fresh air to me on this trip. I never realised it, but I
was getting stale—cynical. Oh, I could still *see* what
would make a good film, I could still recognise a good

subject. But only with my mind. The feeling, the emotion, the involvement—they'd all got less and less. And a director can't manage without them. They put the heart into a film and if they're not there, it shows—however slick and professional his work may be.' He paused and kissed her again, holding her close. 'Seeing your reactions to California showed me just what I was missing,' he murmured. 'Everything was new to you and you weren't ashamed to show it. That look in your eyes when you saw the Golden Gate; your laughter at the magician on Fisherman's Wharf, the magic you brought with you on that cable-car ride. And the day you actually found yourself sitting next to a real live sheriff in a roadside café! I couldn't take my eyes off you, Jessica. I was afraid that every time I looked away you'd see something fresh and I'd miss those stars in your eyes. And after a while I knew I couldn't afford to do that. Ever. I need your stars, Jessica. I need your delight in life. So—what's your answer?' His lips brushed hers and she quivered in his arms. 'Make it yes, Jessica,' he murmured against her mouth.

But there was no need for her to say anything. Her lips gave him their answer in an older way; and as they clung together and the water roared by close to their feet, they slipped from the smoothness of the rock and lay together on the springing moss, hands and lips and bodies entwined as they pledged themselves to each other. High above, the stars wheeled where the turkey vulture had long gone to its roost, deep in the Yosemite, raccoons and ringtails hunted for food while, higher up, black bears stretched themselves after their winter sleep, coyotes howled and mule deer browsed and drowsed uneasily. But Matt and Jessica were aware of none of this. They were aware only of a wild beating roar that might have been the water or might have been their own surging blood as they let their bodies do what they would, and afterwards lay close in each other's arms, planning their lives for what seemed eternal bliss.

Only it hadn't been, had it? Jessica tossed once again and discovered that her pillow was soaked with tears. Oh—hell *damn* the man! Why did he have to come back now and turn her whole life upside down again like this? Why couldn't he just have *stayed away*?

Furious with herself as much as with him, she snapped on the light and threw back the bedclothes. Obviously, she was going to get no sleep at all tonight. She might just as well try to do some work.

Not that that was any way of forgetting Matt. But it might help to put him in his proper place.

CHAPTER THREE

THERE was a good deal of planning to do before Jessica could actually begin work on the new film, and she worked closely with Chris in deciding how to begin her researches. An interview with Emlyn Thomas was fixed for the end of the week and Jessica read his book *A Cottage in Wales* again more thoroughly, poring over the scenes she wanted to dramatise. She intended to work with Emlyn Thomas on the script itself, but there were other factors to think of too, and she decided to get in touch with the casting director, in London, as soon as possible to arrange for the actors. Before that, she would have to know just when filming was to take place, and this in itself depended on a multitude of other things—the prime difficulty being the cottage which was to be burned in the final scene.

Chris was still doubtful about this, although he had said no more to Jessica about it, and he agreed when she suggested they should take a few days next week to look around for locations. 'After we've seen Emlyn Thomas,' she said. 'He may have some ideas himself— he knows the area, after all. Hilary's going to be production assistant, isn't she?'

'Yes, that's right. D'you want her to fix up some accommodation?'

'Mm, but not until we've seen Emlyn Thomas. Get her to stand by on the day we've seen him—if he's got any suggestions we'll fit in with them.' Jessica frowned at her notebook. 'I shall be glad when we can get under way—I always hate this stage, when nothing's decided and nothing *can* be decided. Once we begin, things will start to get clearer, but at present it's like looking at a

41

great pile of jigsaw pieces and not knowing what the picture's supposed to be!'

'Not quite that bad,' Chris grinned. 'You've got some idea of your final picture, after all. What you don't know is where you're going to get the pieces from.'

'And is that supposed to be a comfort?' The phone on Jessica's desk rang and she picked it up, stiffening at once as she heard the caller's voice. 'Oh, hullo, Matt. Yes, I can come along now, if you want me. I was just having a talk with Chris——' She made a face and put down the phone a little harder than necessary. 'You know, that man's just plain *rude*! He doesn't even wait for an answer—just issues his summons and hangs up. Well, I suppose I'll have to run along like a good girl. Thank God he's going away soon!'

'What is it he's doing?' Chris enquired. 'Another *Nature Search*?'

'No, that's finished now. I don't know what this new thing is. Something very highbrow and minority-interest, no doubt!' Jessica stuffed some papers into her shoulder-bag and pushed her chair under her desk. 'I still don't really understand why he wanted to come slumming it at Mercia. But ours is not to reason why, is it? See you, Chris.'

In spite of her nonchalant words, Jessica's heart was thumping as she walked along the corridor to Matt's office, and she cursed herself for her weakness. All right, so he was still nominally her husband—but she hadn't admitted that he had any rights over her for four years now. She'd left him, lived alone, made her own way—and been reasonably successful. So why did she find herself acting like a schoolgirl whenever she had to see him?

Well, it seemed that she didn't have any control over her reactions to Matt—but that didn't mean she had to let him know how he affected her. She paused at his door and took several deep breaths before knocking, then went in looking as cool as she knew how.

'Ah, Jessica.' Matt stood up to greet her, looking as calm and immaculate as ever, and Jessica wondered if there were any emotions at all beneath that glossy exterior. There had been once . . . but she caught herself up sharply. It did *no good* to let herself think like that.

Forcing herself to meet his eyes, she moved forward. He was looking extra smart today, she noticed, and wondered why he should be wearing an obviously expensive light suit to the office, where most people dressed casually. His dark hair was freshly-cut too, though no one had ever been able to tame the springing curls, and her fingers flexed involuntarily at the memory of the feel of them. She caught his eyes on her then in a bright sardonic glance, and looked down hastily, noticing the gleam of dull gold at his wrist. Yes, Matt Fenwood had certainly done well for himself, with his documentaries and his own production company. But then that had always been his ambition, hadn't it?

'I'm glad you could come in,' Matt remarked, just as if he hadn't virtually ordered her to drop everything and come running. 'I just wanted to go over your plans for the film before I leave, and——'

'Leave?' The word bit out more sharply than Jessica had intended, and she saw the dark eyebrows quirk up.

'Yes, I'm away today,' he informed her laconically. 'Flying from Birmingham to Heathrow. So there won't be another chance to talk for some time.'

Thank goodness, Jessica thought, but there was an odd little ache somewhere when she thought of not seeing him again. 'I'm still not sure what it is you're doing,' she confessed. 'Nobody seems to know much about it.'

'That's because the rest of the team are already on their way. We're filming an archaeological dig in Africa—someone's come up with an interesting theory about some remains that were found there a few years ago. Nobody could do much about it until now, there was a lot of unrest in that part, but the present ruler's keen to have some publicity—it's one of these small states one never hears of until they have a revolution or some other claim to fame. In this case, it could be something very interesting to do with man's own origins. It's all been a bit hush-hush, that's why nobody knows too much about it.'

'I see. It sounds fascinating.' Jessica gazed at him. So that was why he was in a lightweight suit. 'And everyone else has already gone?'

'Yes, all except Chantal and myself. We're flying out together—we should be able to make good use of the flight-time in planning, and——'

'Chantal? You mean Chantal Gordon?'

'The anthropologist, yes.' Matt looked amused and Jessica felt herself flush. Why ever had she burst out like that? As if it could be of the slightest interest to her who Matt was working with—or flying with. Anyway, it was easy enough to see why he was keen to do this film—Chantal Gordon was known as the most glamorous anthropologist ever to tread the earth. Tall, willowy, with long blonde hair, she had been seen frequently on television; and the gossip columns were filled with her activities when she wasn't being an anthropologist.

In fact, she was just the kind of woman Matt liked.

Conscious that he was still watching her, Jessica pulled herself together and took out the notes she had made on the film about the Welsh cottage. She laid them on Matt's desk and sat down, indicating in every way she could that this was a business meeting and time was limited.

'Chris and I have sketched out a few ideas,' she began. 'We're seeing Emlyn Thomas on Friday, and depending on his own ideas we'll be looking for film locations next week. Once we've got some idea of the possibilities there we can think about casting, and Chris is finding some other people to interview too. It's beginning to take shape.'

'I see.' Matt picked up the sheets of paper and studied them. 'Have you picked on your scenes for dramatisation yet?'

Jessica bit her lip. She'd been hoping he wouldn't ask that—Chris's reaction to her plan to film the burning of the cottage had been a hint that Matt, too, might think it too expensive. Not that it was up to anyone but her, she reminded herself quickly. It was her business how the budget was allocated—so long as it didn't go over the top.

Matt was waiting for an answer, so she said quickly: 'I haven't made a final choice yet. I want to use both couples, of course, and we'll need to find a suitable cottage. It depends on that, really.'

'Hm.' Matt gave her a thoughtful look and Jessica bent her head, hoping that his talent for reading her mind might fail him on this occasion. 'All right, it seems that you've got things under way. I understand that it all seems a bit nebulous at this stage. No doubt you'll have a lot more to report when I come back.'

'I hope to have a finished film to show you then,' said Jessica, adding belatedly, 'How long do you expect to be away?'

'Could be a couple of months. Yes, you might well have a film for me by then. A rough one, anyway. Now, the main thing I wanted to say, Jessica, is this— remember to keep a balanced view on this subject. It's a highly-emotive one—that's why it makes good television—and it won't be any good if you don't have your own strong feelings about it. But don't let them carry you away, okay?'

Jessica felt indignation blaze through her. Who did he think he was, patronising her this way? Talking as if she'd never directed a film before! 'You don't have to worry, Matt,' she said icily. 'I think I can manage to stay rational, even if I am a woman.'

'Ouch!' Matt said with a grin. 'You'll never let me forget what I once said about women directors, will

you! Don't be so touchy, Jessica. I'm only saying what
it's my job to say.'

'And *I'll* only do what it's my job to do,' she retorted.
'I'm not in this business to make propaganda.'

'That's all right, then,' he said, unabashed. 'So long
as we understand each other. I think you can make a
good job of this film, Jessica. You've got good material
to start with, anyway. And Emlyn Thomas' book is a
masterpiece—with that in your hand, you can't go
wrong.'

'Thank you,' Jessica said coolly, and there was a tiny
silence. 'Well, if that's all you wanted me for——'

Matt stopped her as she began to gather her notes
together. 'Wait a minute, Jessica. That wasn't all I
wanted you for, as it happens. There was something else
I wanted to discuss, too.' He moved round the desk
towards her. 'You're not in a hurry, are you?'

She faced him, her throat suddenly dry. She sought
wildly for an excuse to get out, but could think of
nothing. 'I—I ought to be getting back,' she said
lamely. 'There might be a phone call——'

'And there might not. And if there is, someone else
will answer it.' He was close now, close enough for
Jessica to feel the warmth of his body through the
lightweight suit. His breath touched her cheek, and she
shivered and moved away.

'Don't go, Jessica.' Matt put out one hand and touched
her chin with a long forefinger. 'I told you before, we
have things to discuss. I'd like to discuss them before I
go away.'

'Then I'm afraid you've left it too late,' she told him,
hoping that he wouldn't notice the shake in her voice. 'I
haven't got time to discuss anything now, and *I* told
you that there was nothing for us to discuss anyway.
We've been apart four years now, Matt, we've each
made our own lives and as far as I'm concerned that's
all there is to it.'

'As far as you're concerned?' he mocked her. 'And

do I have no say at all? It does concern me too, you know.'

'I really don't see what there is to say,' Jessica exclaimed impatiently. 'Let me go, Matt. We're nothing to each other any more—can't you accept that?'

Matt slid his hand under her chin and let the fingers trail down her slim neck, the tips coming to rest just below her collarbone. With his other hand he drew her towards him and, before she could resist, pulled her hard against his body and kissed her—not gently, tenderly as he had on that first night in California, but fiercely, demandingly, as if he were trying to force her to submit. Jessica gasped and jerked her head back, but he was holding her too strongly and she felt their teeth clash together, tasted the blood on her soft inner lip and gave a whimper of pain as he crushed her breasts against the rock of his chest.

The first fierce onslaught lasted for seconds only; then his lips softened and gentled, caressing hers with a sensuous tenderness that had her weak and trembling, moving in an exploration that compelled its own response. Jessica swayed in his arms, taken completely by surprise and unable to hide her reactions. She slid her arms around his body, clinging to him, knowing that she would fall without his support, knowing that her own body would betray her and unable to do a thing about it. And she wasn't even sure any more that it mattered. There was nothing—nothing in the world— but this, her body close to Matt's, her mouth and his telling their own story, her hands in his hair and his moving surely and confidently over her, drawing her to greater heights, reminding her of all that she had missed and yearned for in the past four long, lonely years. . . .

'Nothing to each other any more?' he whispered against her ear. 'Can *you* accept that, Jessica?'

Jessica rested her head against his chest, unable to answer. Her blood pounded, the roaring in her ears all but drowned his voice, and her tongue felt too bruised to speak. She was shaken to the roots by what had happened. Had she never realised that she was missing Matt—that it was longing for his kisses that kept her awake at nights, a deep yearning for his caress, for the feeling of his body hard against hers, that created that empty void? Had she been fooling herself all this time—telling herself that she was happy and fulfilled, when all along she'd been deeply and miserably frustrated?

'Now do you say we've nothing to discuss?' Matt murmured, and he bent his head to hers again.

But the kiss had scarcely begun when a knock on the door sent them both apart, Jessica to the side of the room, Matt blinking and startled by his desk. After a brief pause the knock sounded again; and then, before Matt could respond, the door opened and Jessica saw a woman standing there. A tall, slender woman with a willowy figure and long blonde hair that curled around her perfect, oval face, making a frame for full red lips and huge turquoise eyes.

Chantal Gordon. It had to be.

'Matt!' Chantal's voice was as soft and silky as her appearance. 'Didn't you hear me knock! I thought you must be out, but a little girl in the main office told me you were here.' She came forward, every movement as sinuous as that of a sleek Siamese cat, and caught Matt lightly by the lapels while she kissed him. 'Nearly ready, darling? I don't want to be late checking in at the airport.'

Matt stood quite still, looking down at her. He seemed to have forgotten about Jessica as he smiled and answered: 'Always ready where you're concerned, Chantal. But I've just a little unfinished business to attend to here—if you don't mind hanging on.' He turned and stretched a hand out to Jessica. 'Have you met Jessica? We've just been talking over one of the films in my social conditions series.'

Chantal turned slowly and stared at Jessica, who was

trembling with reaction and indignation in her corner. Unfinished business, indeed! Was *that* all she was? And to think she'd nearly fallen for it—nearly fallen for Matt, all over again! God, when was she going to learn? When was she going to realise that with Matt physical attraction was all there was? He might have ten times his fair share—but he had nothing else, that was for sure. Nothing in the way of depth, integrity, real genuine feeling.

'Jessica?' Chantal was examining her as if she were some rare form of humanity. She'll be able to write a thesis on me if she stares much harder, Jessica thought bitterly. 'Oh yes, weren't you and Matt married once? I've heard about you.' She made it sound as if Jessica were something boring and half-forgotten mentioned briefly at school.

'Matt and I still *are* married,' Jessica said coldly, although this was a fact she rarely acknowledged. 'We just haven't lived together for a while. Over four years, actually.'

'Really? Waiting for the magic five?' Chantal smiled up into Matt's face. 'How very civilised of you both. And you've even given Jessica a job, too. So much better than bitter wrangling, isn't it?'

'I'm directing a film Matt's producing, yes,' said Jessica, even more coldly. 'We were just going over some of the details.' Feeling more sure of herself now, she let her hazel eyes rest on Matt's face. 'He mentioned some unfinished business, didn't he?'

'Well, don't let me interrupt you.' Chantal sat down in one of the low chairs, crossing elegant legs. Anything less like an anthropologist she'd never seen, Jessica thought, taking in the fashionable green suit that showed off every shapely line of the other woman's body. Though she probably looked different in the field. But even in jeans and a T-shirt, that wonderful hair and those huge eyes would stand out. And nothing could make that willowy figure look lumpy.

'I—I think we'd finished, actually,' Jessica faltered, looking at Matt, whose impassive face gave her no clues. What *was* he thinking? she wondered despairingly. Was he regretting the interruption—or did he really look on her merely as 'unfinished business'? The tenderness she'd felt in his kiss—was it real? Or just a sample of his expertise, calculatingly designed to make her succumb to his charm? And if so, what for? So that he could humiliate her all over again?

Well, he wasn't going to get the chance. Once was enough, and she was almost glad that Chantal had brought their little scene to an end. Otherwise there was no knowing what would have happened. She must make sure that there were no other scenes like that between her and Matt—not that there was much danger, with him about to go off for several weeks in Africa with Chantal. By the time they returned, no doubt his interest would be concentrated entirely on the beautiful anthropologist and he would have no time to spare for Jessica.

'Yes, I think we had finished, more or less,' he drawled, and Jessica wanted to hit him. 'Well, good luck, Jessica. I'm sure you'll cope, and don't forget Graham's my co-producer, and he'll be around if any snags arise. And I'll see you when I get back.'

'Yes, all right,' she murmured, and watched as Chantal took Matt's arm. They looked good together, she thought detachedly; the blonde head only a few inches below the dark, the slender voluptuousness of the woman complemented by the lean sensuality of the man. If they weren't already lovers, it was unreasonable to suppose that they wouldn't be soon, under that hot African sun.

So what was it Matt had wanted to discuss with her, that needed a kiss to start it? What was he trying to prove when he held her in his arms?

Jessica and Chris went together to interview Emlyn

Thomas. It was part of the researcher's job to act as a back-up to the director's line of thought, working in the same way but often thinking of different angles and fresh points of view. In this way the subject could be dealt with more thoroughly and points covered that might otherwise be missed.

With Matt away, not only from the office but from the country, Jessica was able to concentrate more fully on her task, though she still found his face creeping into her mind at moments when she least expected it, and the memory of his kisses still made her shiver. When this happened, she turned her mind sternly to work, and was thankful to find that it was sufficiently interesting to absorb her thoughts without too much difficulty.

Emlyn Thomas lived near Dolgellau, about sixty miles from Shrewsbury, and the country roads were quiet as Chris drove away from the old town and headed for Wales. Jessica sat beside him, watching the scenery pass, and thinking about the book. She had read it again last night and the powerful emotions of the characters were still with her. In a way, it was a pity it had never been turned into a complete TV play—but for her own sake, she was glad it hand't. The chance to use such a book, by such a writer, was like a gift from the gods, and she wondered for the first time just how Matt had been able to arrange it.

They crossed the winding Severn at Welshpool and the scenery became wilder, the hills more rugged. Around Shrewsbury, the country was flat and mild; here, it was untamed, craggy mountains rising abruptly from the roadside, covered in parts with a blanket of dark green conifers, in others too hostile to accept any plant life other than the clinging lichen. Jessica craned her neck, awed. No wonder the Welsh themselves were intransigent and difficult to tame; an environment like this must have an effect on the personality, must make it as rugged as the rocks themselves.

It was almost eleven when they finally arrived at

Emlyn Thomas's house, a long, low farmhouse of stone
and slate with a view of the huge humped shoulder of
Cader Idris from its sitting-room window. Jessica got
out of the car and stared around, overwhelmed by the
grandeur of the surroundings, the towering mountains,
the distant peaks. Below in the valley lay the little town
of Dolgellau, which she had already learnt to
pronounce as Dolgethly, and she knew that the river
which began to broaden at just that point would, in a
few miles, widen to become the beautiful Mawddach
Estuary at Barmouth.

'Like it then, do you?' Jessica jumped slightly and
turned to smile at the man who had come quietly to the
gate to greet them. So this was Emlyn Thomas! He was
instantly recognisable from the photograph on the
jacket of his books—tall, broad, with a thatch of white
hair waving back from a high forehead, and twinkling
blue eyes under shaggy brows. His square face was lined,
but the lines were all cheerful ones and there was
humour as well as keenness in his glance.

'It's beautiful,' she told him sincerely. 'And it's very
good of you to let us come. I'm Jessica Fenwood, and
this is Chris Kirk.'

They shook hands and she liked the firm grasp. A
feeling of relief swept over her. A lot had depended on
this first meeting. If she and Emlyn hadn't got on,
things would have been very difficult.

'Come in, then.' The Welsh lilt was faint but
unmistakable as he turned to lead them into the house.
'Mair's got some coffee on the stove—I expect you'd
like a cup, wouldn't you? Just settle yourselves down in
here while I go and tell her you've arrived.'

Jessica and Chris found themselves in a large sitting-
room, comfortably furnished with the chintzy cottage-
style furniture that went so well with the Welsh
building. The big window along one wall was like a
living picture, with Cader Idris green and massive
against a blue sky. Jessica crossed to look at it, while

Chris roamed about looking at the books on the shelves and examining some old engravings on the wall.

'Well, I see you're looking at our view.' Emlyn Thomas was back, ushering in a small, plump woman with dark hair who was carrying a tray of coffee. 'Fine, isn't it? Not that we get such a good sight of it as this all the time, you know. The mist blots it right out, as often as not.'

'Wales certainly doesn't seem to be living up to its reputation today,' Chris agreed. 'Not a raincloud in sight. I should think you get more than your fair share here, don't you?'

'Oh, we get enough, we get enough.' Emlyn pulled forward some armchairs and grouped them around the window. 'We'll sit and enjoy it while we've got it, shall we? This is my wife, Mair, by the way. Anything you want to know about me, just ask her—she knows all my secrets.'

Mrs Thomas smiled at them and poured out the coffee. She was evidently quite accustomed to her husband's sense of humour and bore a good deal of gentle teasing with no more than a scolding glance before she excused herself and left them to their discussion. Jessica watched her go with some envy. It was quite clear that the Thomases enjoyed a happy and companionable marriage, and she wondered a little sadly what the secret might be.

'So now,' said Emlyn, draining his cup and refilling it before sitting back in his chair, 'what exactly are you planning to do to my book?'

'I hope we're not going to do anything *to* it,' Jessica said, with a quick glance at Chris. 'But as you know, we'd like to use it in a documentary about the Welsh cottage situation. Some of the scenes, dramatised, would make certain points better than any amount of interviews or statistics—though we'll be including them, too. So we want to discuss those scenes with you, and we'd also like to talk about the situation generally. You must know as much about it as almost anyone.'

'Yes, I suppose I probably do,' Emlyn said thoughtfully. 'I've seen so much of it, see. Oh, I know it could be said I'm part of it myself—living in this old farmhouse. But it was derelict, you know, when I bought it. Nobody local would have had the money to do it up, it would have just rotted away. So I like to think I've brought it back into the community. But these little cottages—that's a different story.' He stared out of the window at the looming mountain and shook his fine head.

'They're not derelict, then,' Jessica prompted him.

'Well, sometimes they are, of course—but no, usually they're just nice little cottages, farmworkers' cottages, or quarrymen's, that kind of thing. Two up, two down and a lean-to kitchen at the back, you know. Just right for a young couple just starting out in life, and right for a family too. There's been many a family brought up in those cottages.' Jessica remembered that Emlyn Thomas himself had come from quite a poor family and if he had not grown up in a tiny farm cottage had probably lived in something very like it. 'And it wasn't so bad, you know,' he added, obviously deep in his own memories. 'Life was pretty hard, but it could be good too. There's a lot to be said for a big family, even if it does keep you poor.'

'What do you think has changed, then, with regard to the cottages?' Chris asked.

'Oh well, it was all the affluent society a few years ago, wasn't it? People in the cities earning more than they knew what to do with. They had their big cars and their televisions and their holidays abroad, they sent their kids to private schools, and then they looked round for something else to spend it on. And they wanted an investment, too. What better than a little country cottage? Especially as they were so cheap at that time, with the local people having to go to the towns for work. It started small at first—a few people, buying up a little place for weekends, doing it up nice. Then more people started to do it too and the farmers and landowners realised they were on to a good thing. They put up the prices—you can't blame them—and what with that and the way property prices soared a few years ago, it soon reached the stage where nobody local could afford to buy a place at all. And that's when the resentment started to creep in. It's quite understandable. Only it didn't stop there. The Welsh aren't famous for taking things lying down—they've had to fight too much all through their history—and it wasn't long before someone went out one night with a few matches and some petrol and started a little fire. And then someone else did the same—and so it spread. But it's all in the book.'

'Yes, and very movingly too.' Jessica hesitated, then asked, 'The young man—Huw—was he based on anyone in particular?'

Emlyn gave her a sharp glance. 'What makes you ask that?'

'I'm not really sure,' she confessed. 'I could say it's because he seems so real—but all your characters do. But there's something extra about Huw. He seems almost to jump off the page. It's so tragic, what happens to him. He loses everything.'

'Yes, he does.' Emlyn rubbed his chin reflectively, then turned his eyes on her. There was little humour in them now; they were sharp, incisive, and reminded her in an odd way of Matt's. 'And what would you say if I told you he was real? What would you want to do?'

'I think I'd want to interview him,' Jessica said truthfully.

'Yes, I imagined you'd say that.' Emlyn thought again. 'Let's just say he's drawn from a more general picture of life,' he said at last. 'There are a lot of young men about like Huw—setting out in life, seeing it all laid out before them—then seeing their dreams shattered one by one, until, as you say, they've got nothing left. Huw could be any one of those.'

Jessica wanted to say, *But he's not, is he?* It was clear from Emlyn's reaction to her question that Huw was as real as she was herself, though Emlyn might well have developed his story for the book. But she knew that it was no good pressing the matter, though she badly wanted to speak to the young man now that she knew he existed. Emlyn didn't yet know her well enough to be sure that she could be trusted; he might change his mind later. In any case, he wasn't a man who would be open to persuasion.

'Can you tell me something about the research you did for the book?' she asked. 'You must have talked to quite a lot of people, on both sides. Or all three, I suppose—the landowners who sold the cottages, the city people who bought them, the locals who were robbed of the chance to buy their own homes and had to leave the district altogether, like Huw and Olwen.'

'Oh yes, I talked to quite a lot. I already knew a good bit, of course, just from living here. It's a tragic thing, you know. It robs the village of its heart if half the houses are empty most of the time, just used by strangers for weekends. The community dies. There aren't enough people to support a local industry, there aren't enough children to keep the school open. The church and chapel are empty and the social life that goes with them dies away. Bus services don't pay, so they stop, and the lack of transport brings other problems for the people who do live there; they can't get to work in the nearest town, so they move out too. There aren't enough sick to keep a doctor busy, or a chemist's shop. There may not be enough for a shop of any kind, and even the mobile library might find it's not worthwhile calling. So gradually, over the years, the place withers away. The only people who can afford to live there are the ones with cars to take them to their work. There are plenty of little villages now that are virtually deserted during the day.'

'But that's horrifying,' Jessica said slowly, and the fine white head nodded.

'That's what my book is trying to say. But you have to see the other side as well. The city businessman from Birmingham or Coventry has the money. He has a need to get away, to enjoy the fresh air and the hills, to recuperate from the strains of his rat-race of a life. He wants his children to know something other than city streets and hard pavements. It's an escape, but it's an escape that's vitally necessary to him. Who is going to tell him that he doesn't have the right to buy himself a little cottage somewhere, if he can afford it? And is it his fault that the farmer asks a high price? He probably doesn't even realise it *is* a high price.'

'It isn't even the farmer's fault, is it?' said Jessica. 'He may be in desperate need just to keep his farm going, as in your book. Or the cottage may be privately sold, by some relation who doesn't live in the district any more, who's inherited the property perhaps from an old parent, and just wants the best price he can get.'

'Oh yes,' Emlyn agreed, 'there are as many points of view as there are people. All you have to do is sort out the ones you want to represent.'

Shocked, Jessica looked at him. The bright blue eyes were watching her steadily. 'But I want to present a balanced view,' she said. 'I'm not taking sides.'

'No? It's a highly emotive subject, and you're a sensitive person. Will you be able to remain completely detached?'

'No, probably not,' she answered honestly. 'But I don't really have to. A director *should* feel involved with the subject. That's different from being biased.'

'Yes, of course. Well, why don't you both come along to my study and I'll show you some of my research notes. I've got photos too, there might be something you can use there.'

Over lunch some time later the talk turned from the
documentary aspect to the dramatisation. 'What kind
of actors would you have in mind?' asked Jessica.
'Anyone special? Or any special type?'

Emlyn considered. 'I think that's something I'll have
to leave to you,' he said. 'Young Huw, for instance, he
needs to be very sensitively played. He starts off as a
quiet, decent young chap and he's driven to his limits
by what happens—having to move to the city, Olwen
losing the baby, everything blamed on the loss of that
cottage. I wouldn't like to see him seem to become a
whiner, blaming everyone else for his misfortunes. He
really does suffer a lot before he takes that drastic step,
but you're not going to have too much time to show
that, are you?'

'Not in the scenes we use, no. But the documentary
inserts will compensate. We're using the drama to
illustrate points made in documentary, rather than the
other way about. I don't think Huw will show up badly.
Of course, it all depends on who's free when we film.
It's no good having any fixed ideas beforehand.'

'And when will that be?'

'Well, I'd like it to be next month. We'll have to find
a cottage before then—or two cottages. Once that's
organised, we shall be able to make more definite plans.
The documentary filming can be fitted around that.'

'Two cottages?' asked Mair Thomas, putting some
more potatoes on Chris's plate.

'Yes—we need a derelict one that's going to be
demolished anyway, for the fire scene, and a real
holiday cottage, one that's been nicely modernised, for
interior shots.' Jessica turned to Emlyn. 'Do you have
any ideas where we might find them?'

Emlyn stroked his chin. 'A derelict cottage? Won't
that present a few problems?'

'I don't think so, provided we can get the local
authority's agreement to the fire. We have to have all
the services standing by, of course—fire, ambulance and

so on. They have to be paid for—don't want anyone complaining about a burden on the rates! And we'll probably have to do it up a bit on the outside if it's very derelict, just to make sure that it looks habitable. But stone cottages look fairly good almost up to the last moment, don't they? No, the biggest problem is finding one.'

'Hm. I'll have a think. There may be something not too far away. And I don't imagine you'll have much trouble in finding the modernised one.'

'No, I shouldn't think so.' Jessica glanced at Chris. 'I can't think of any more just now, can you?'

Chris shook his head. 'No, we've plenty to go on now. Though it would be helpful if you could come up with any ideas about the cottages. Otherwise it means a tour round the local authorities to find any that are condemned, followed by visits.' He made a rueful face. 'Something like house-hunting but rather more depressing!'

'I'll give it some thought,' Emlyn promised, and then, as Mair served them with apple pie, he changed the subject. 'And how's Matt? I hear he's off to Africa.'

Jessica's heart lurched at the unexpected mention of his name, but she answered calmly enough. 'Yes, he's gone to do a programme with Chantal Gordon about some old remains that have been found there. They're all very excited about it, I believe.'

'And he's left you in charge.' The blue eyes looked at her and she wondered just how much he knew. That she and Matt were married, for instance? He seemed to know Matt quite well, though she didn't recall Matt having mentioned him during their brief time together. He must have realised that their names were the same, though, and not for the first time she wished she had gone back to her maiden name for professional use.

'The director always is left in charge,' she replied coolly. 'The producer doesn't interfere after he's given the first outline, unless on matters of policy or budget.

He approves the film when it's made, or suggests a different layout, but he doesn't interfere with the actual making.'

'I see. I've always been a little confused about the difference between a producer and director.' Emlyn spoke solemnly, and Jessica knew that many people shared this confusion, but she wasn't at all sure that Emlyn really was one of them. Still, it didn't really matter. She was dealing with him as herself, director of the film, not as Matt's wife.

'I'd like to go over those scenes I've picked out, if you don't mind,' she said. 'If we could rough out a script I'll get it typed and let you have a copy. Could we do that this afternoon?'

'By all means. Mair, we'll have our coffee in the study, I think, so we can get on.' Emlyn rose to his feet. 'Are you going to be helping with this, Chris?'

Chris shook his head. 'I think two are better on that kind of job. I'll go for a walk—have a look around. I might find one or two nice locations, or views. We'll be needing a few atmospheric shots.'

'Oh, you'll get them right enough.' Emlyn stood back while Chris carried some dishes out to the kitchen for Mair, then he turned to Jessica. 'Come along, then. You've had a long journey to get here and we want to make the most of your time.'

It was almost dark when, after a hearty Welsh tea of *bara brith*, scones, Welsh cakes and plank bread, Jessica and Chris set off for the drive back to Shrewsbury. They were waved off by Emlyn and Mair, and Jessica had the warm feeling of having made new friends. Emlyn Thomas had all the qualities of a good writer; insight, compassion and the ability to see and present all sides of a question. At the same time he was clearly deeply involved with the problems he wrote about, and convinced that he was, in the best way he could, doing his best to alleviate them by bringing them to public notice. And he could do that while still giving his readers something that entertained; a believable story. A picture.

But she still couldn't help wondering just how and when he had met Matt. She had been conscious, once or twice, of the sharp blue eyes resting on her reflectively; as if he, too, were wondering. Was he wondering what had happened between her and Matt? Why they had broken up—perhaps even why they had married in the first place? Or had Matt given Emlyn his own version, whatever that was, and was Emlyn trying to match this with his own ideas?

Jessica sighed. That was something she would never know. What surprised her was the fact that she wanted to. Wouldn't it be better if she stopped herself from indulging in this pointless speculation?

Wouldn't it have been better still if Matt had never come back into her life?

CHAPTER FOUR

Once work had begun on the planning for the film, things began to fall into place. One of Jessica's first tasks was to arrange for the casting, and she drew up a list of requirements for the casting director in London; he would search out all those who seemed to display the right characteristics and arrange for Jessica to meet them. That would probably mean a couple of days in London at least, she thought, and made a note to remind Hilary to fix accommodation for her.

Meanwhile, Chris had gone to Wales to look for cottages. Nothing more had been heard from Emlyn Thomas, but he had promised to let them know immediately if he had any news of suitable locations. In the meantime, he was happy to let Jessica polish up the script they had roughed out. She hadn't asked him any more about the 'real' Huw, guessing that while he was unlikely to forget he wouldn't like being pressed. If he did decide to allow her to meet the young Welshman, he would let her know. In any case, it would depend on 'Huw' himself—whoever he really was, he might have strong and quite understandable reasons for not wanting to be interviewed on television.

Of Matt, somewhere in Africa with Chantal Gordon, there was no word. But she hadn't expected any—had she?

'The only thing I'm a bit worried about,' Chris had said before he left, 'is the budget. This fire scene—it's going to cost a mint, you know.'

'Then we'll just have to make room for it,' Jessica told him. 'That scene's *important*, Chris. It'll be the climax of the whole film. We can't do without it.'

Chris looked as if he might argue, but changed his

mind. 'All right,' he shrugged, 'you're the director. So I'm to look for two cottages, yes?'

'Yes, fairly near to each other if possible. And a similar construction, of course—the inside of the good one's got to look as if it could be the derelict one outside, if you see what I mean. And if we can make it look decent without spending too much—you see, I am thinking of the budget!'

Chris grunted, then smiled. He really was rather attractive, Jessica thought, looking at his thick fair hair, growing all ways over his head, and his mild blue eyes. It was a pity he and Sue had broken up. It seemed to happen so much in this business. . . . On an impulse, she laid her hand over his and said, 'How's Jasper, Chris? Have you seen him lately?'

'Jasper?' Chris looked at her for a moment, almost as if wondering who she meant. 'Oh, he's fine. Walking everywhere—a real little tough. I saw him last weekend, as a matter of fact.'

'And Sue?' Jessica probed delicately. She didn't want to pry, but she wanted to let Chris know that if he needed to talk she was ready to listen. But Chris just shrugged, his blue eyes going blank.

'No change. If I change my job, she might change her mind, but not otherwise. And that's it.'

'Change your job? But you're so good at it! And you'll get promotion before long—you'll be a director yourself, a producer. Are you thinking of it, Chris? It's a lot to ask—what would you do?'

'No idea. I suppose there are things I could do, but none of them appeal to me much—the nine-to-five sort of jobs that Sue'd want me to take. And the things I wouldn't mind—well, they'd all have much the same effect. Long hours, and a lot of time away from home. I guess I must just be that sort of man.'

'I suppose it depends on how much value you place on your marriage,' Jessica said thoughtfully, but Chris shook his head.

'It's not that simple, is it? Everything else being equal, I'd do anything to save me and Sue. I didn't want a break-up. Believe me, Jessica, I've thought about it, I've thought about it a lot. I've tried to imagine myself doing one of those executive jobs, the plushy office, the company car, the expense account lunches. Going off each morning with my briefcase, home for dinner every evening. And it would do something to me, Jessica. I wouldn't be the same person. However hard I tried, I wouldn't be able to stop the damage, and it would affect Sue and me just like a corrosive acid. It would wreck us just as surely—more surely—than this has. As we are now, there's still hope. If that happened, there'd be none at all, and I'd have lost everything—Sue, my marriage, Jasper, and myself.' He paused, looking past Jessica. 'My job might not be of world-shaking importance to anyone else, but it's important to me. It suits the way I am. It lets me *be* the way I am. That's what's important, and that's what nobody's got the right to change. Do you understand that, Jessica?'

Jessica stared at him. *Letting people be the way they are*—that was what was important. Had that caused the split, the deep irrevocable chasm, between her and Matt? Hadn't they been satisfied to let each other be the way they were—be themselves, true to their own natures? She had never thought of it in quite that way before, and this wasn't really the time to think about it now, with Chris's blue eyes fixed on her with a kind of strained anxiety.

'Yes, I think I do understand,' she said slowly. 'You're right, Chris. We have to be the way we are—if we try to be anything different, something will have to give. Like putting feet into the wrong shoes. You end up with corns or bunions, or else the shoes split.'

He grinned suddenly and relaxed. 'Trust you to bring me down to earth, Jessica! Well, as far as Sue was concerned, I was a pair of Wellingtons about three sizes too big. We met where we touched, and that just wasn't good enough—for Sue, anyway. And why should I try to force her to live her life in a second-class way?'

Jessica shook her head. There didn't seem to be any answer. She'd always thought Chris and Sue an ideal couple and had been shocked and upset when they split up. It was, she knew, one of the occupational hazards of working in T.V., but in their case surely there had been hope that it might be just temporary. Chris's words now seemed to deny that hope. And everybody— Chris, Sue and, most of all perhaps, little Jasper—was the loser.

Sometimes, life was altogether too difficult. And it wasn't surprising that, later that evening when she was back in her cottage, she should find her mind going back over the break-up of her own marriage.

The first few months had been idyllic, she recalled, unable even now to repress a surge of excitement at the memory of Matt's lovemaking. But she wouldn't allow herself to think about it; with contact re-established between them, it would be all too easy to fall into the pit that desire had dug for her before. That was something she'd sworn would never happen.

But just what had gone wrong? Chris's words came back to her. Had she and Matt tried to change each other, to force each other into moulds—or shoes—that wouldn't fit? Would their marriage have worked if they hadn't, or was it doomed from the start?

She remembered that first quarrel they'd had—the first real one. Matt had come home jubilant with a new assignment—a documentary on Finland, showing it in all its aspects, with plenty of emphasis placed on its countryside and the tiny wilderness huts that dotted its forests, where families would spend their holidays in the seclusion of a landscape that had never been touched by man. Jessica listened, almost as excited as Matt himself—and then the bombshell had burst.

'In July?' she'd echoed when Matt told her the date. 'Oh, no—I won't be able to come.'

'Won't be able to come?' Up to then, Matt had always taken care to book Jessica as his production assistant. 'What on earth do you mean?'.

'What I say.' Jessica's own disappointment made her snappy. 'I'm already tied up for the second week in July. Mike Jennings wants me for the coalmine feature he's doing. It's a nuisance, but there's nothing I can do about it. You'll have to suss out the best places and we'll go for a holiday some time.'

Matt stared at her. 'Jessica, say that again. *Mike Jennings* wants you—for a feature on *coalmines*? Am I dreaming, or something?'

'No, of course not. What's so strange about Mike booking me? We've worked together quite a few times. I've learned a lot from Mike.'

'You have, have you?' Matt was still staring at her, and there was something in his iron-grey eyes that Jessica didn't like.

'Yes, I have, and all of it about direction,' she retorted. 'Just what are you getting at, Matt?'

'Oh, nothing. In any case, it's not that irrevocable. There's plenty of time for Mike to find someone else. I'll see him tomorrow and get it fixed. Oh, and I didn't tell you—the Finnish——'

Jessica cut in without waiting to hear. 'You'll do what? See Mike and get it fixed? Get what fixed—my job? Because it *is* my job, Matt—not just an offshoot of yours, you know.' She was beginning to feel cold. This was their first real quarrel and it could be easily resolved by her giving in and agreeing to go with Matt to Finland. In many ways, it was just what she wanted to do. But there were other issues at stake. 'Don't you think *I* could fix it with Mike, if I wanted to?' she went on, her indignation growing.

Matt looked at her in surprise. 'Well, of course you can, if you'd rather. I just thought it'd be easier for me, as I'm probably going to see him tomorrow. I thought it'd come better over a jar or two at lunchtime. But if you'd rather——'

'No, I *wouldn't* rather,' Jessica said tightly. 'I don't want to "fix" it at all. I only said that if I *wanted* to——'

Matt sighed. 'Let's get this straight, Jessica. Are you saying you don't want to come to Finland with me, or have I lost my place in this argument? And if you don't want to come, why in heaven's name not? I can't believe it's because you've promised Mike Jennings you'll go down a coalmine with him!'

'But it is!' Jessica ran her fingers through her hair, wondering how she could possibly make Matt understand. 'Look, I know we've worked together ever since we got married and quite a bit before—and I've enjoyed it, I'm not saying I haven't. But it can't be good for us always to be on the same jobs. I want to learn— to get on—and the best way for me is to work with several different directors. Can't you see that, Matt?'

'No, quite honestly, I can't. What do you need to learn? You're a very good P.A.—one of the best I've had, as a matter of fact, or I wouldn't want you myself—not as a P.A. anyway,' he added with the quirky leprechaun grin that always got him his way. 'So what else do you want?'

'Well, I don't want to be a P.A. all my life, for one thing,' Jessica told him quietly.

There was a tiny silence. Then Matt said, 'Well, you won't be, will you? We'll be starting a family some time, I suppose.'

'I didn't mean that, Matt. I meant that I want to be a director myself before long.' Jessica raised her hazel eyes, a dark gold now as she tried to make him understand. 'I thought you knew that.'

'A director? Well, I knew you had some thoughts in that line—but we're married now, Jessica. We——'

'And what the hell difference does that make?' The

words exploded from Jessica and with them her body moved so violently that she jerked out of her chair and stood over him, glaring down at his astonished face. 'You haven't taken me over body and soul! It wasn't my ultimate ambition, you know, to be Mrs Matt Fenwood. I still want to be *me*. I still want to achieve as much as I can. Is there something unnatural in that? Something disloyal—unwifely? Something I should have mentioned at the altar?'

'Wind it down, Jessica,' Matt advised, remaining infuriatingly calm. 'There's no need to get all steamed up. All right, so you want to be a director. Well, one day you may be. But in the meantime, I don't see why you shouldn't come to Finland with me. I told you, Mike won't mind——'

'But *I* do! I mind very much. And I mind being patronised and patted on the head and told that perhaps one day, if I'm very good, Santa might let me be a director. I've told you, Matt, I want to make my own way—and I can't do that while you've got your wing over me like a mother chicken!'

Matt's eyes were cold, iron with the frost on it. 'And is that how you see me? Because I want you with me, want to take care of you? Perhaps you'll accuse me of being a mother hen if I tell you that I'm not at all keen on your doing a feature in a coalmine? There are plenty of other things you could be doing, Jessica, things more suitable for a woman. Or am I being over-protective?'

'Yes, as a matter of fact you are.' Jessica forced herself to speak more calmly, but the anger still seethed inside her. 'I'm sorry, Matt, but I intend to get all the experience I can, in as many ways as possible and with as many directors. I want to make a success of my job, and I'll never do that while I'm tied to your apron-strings.' She turned away, aware that this was an important moment in their whole relationship. 'Find another P.A. to go to Finland with you, Matt. I'm going to do the coalmine feature with Mike Jennings, and I'll do any other features that come along. I'm not your private P.A. In fact, I'm not your private property at all!'

The silence was longer this time. Jessica stood with her back to the room, staring fixedly out of the window. She heard no sound at all; but a moment or two later, she felt Matt's body close behind her, and she shivered as his hands came round her waist and curved up over her breasts.

'Not my private property?' Matt murmured in her ear, his voice silky and suggestive. 'Are you sure about that, Jessica?'

Jessica tensed and said nothing. This was always Matt's way of settling an argument; they both knew that once their bodies touched, once their skins met, no quarrel could be sustained. But even as her eyes closed and her hands moved involuntarily to cover his and hold them closer against her, she knew that no sensual delight would make her give way on this. She trembled in Matt's arms, feeling his hardness against her. It wasn't fair—he was using their mutual desire to get his own way. . . .

Well, two could play at that game. Maybe Matt would be the one to give way, in the aftermath of lovemaking. And Jessica sighed and stretched herself back against his firm body, curving her arms over her head and slipping her hands behind Matt's neck to pull him closer, so that his lips nuzzled her neck and she could rub her cheek against his as seductively as her body was moulding itself to his contours, making tiny movements and contacts that brought a groan to his lips and tightened his hands as they moved freely over her taut curves.

'Jessica,' he murmured, deep in his throat. 'Jessica, I love you . . . you're mine, my very own—private property—no one else's. And I'm yours.' With a swift movement, he lifted her to her feet and carried her across the room to the thick rug that covered the floor in front of the glowing fire. He laid her down and leant over her, his face lit by the flames, the grey of his eyes lightened to silver now, a lock of dark hair falling forward over his brow. Shaking, Jessica reached up a hand to smooth it back; he caught her wrist, turning his lips to her palm, then running his mouth along her inner arm from wrist to elbow, burning the delicate skin with kisses of white flame; and then keeping his grip on her hand, stretched her arm above her head and bent his lips to the curved breast outlined beneath her thin cotton shirt.

'We belong to each other,' he breathed, and lowered his body to cover hers, moving sensuously on her so that she could feel every hard line of his response and knew that her own body was now taking control, breasts swelling, nipples tightening, blood surging in a thundering symphony of desire that would now take over and dictate every movement until it had achieved its complete expression.

With a tiny sigh of capitulation, Jessica wound her arms round his neck and let his hands roam where they would, tinglingly exploring the whole of her body, stimulating her to new heights of passion as he always did; each experience surpassing the last until she was convinced there could be no new mountains to climb, no higher peaks to scale.

Arms, legs and bodies entwined, they rocked to and fro on the shaggy rug, feeling its roughness under their bare skins, feeling the warmth of the fire on naked flesh; lips and hands caressed in total and unashamed abandonment as once again they expressed their love and came together in a pulsing rhythm that beat with relentless and increasing speed until finally it exploded in a burst of cries from both their throats, cries that were almost small screams in the near-agony of climax, dying away slowly to whimpers as tiny as the mewing of a newly-born kitten.

'Jessica,' Matt murmured after a long time, when

they had fallen apart and lay exhausted and quiescent, in a tangle of limbs, 'you won't go down that coalmine, will you? Tell me you won't.'

For a brief moment Jessica was tempted to respond as she always had before; to tell him, warm from loving, that of course she wouldn't go down the mine, or any other, that of course she would go with him to Finland and do whatever else he wanted.... But even as she opened her mouth, something stopped her. Wasn't this just what she'd expected? Wasn't it the very reason why Matt had made love to her—so that she'd do as he asked? Or demanded. And hadn't she, in the few moments while she'd still been able to calculate, determined to play him at his own game?

It seemed a mean trick now. But she nuzzled her lips into his neck and whispered: 'Let me do it, Matt. I really do want to.'

'Come with me to Finland,' he breathed, letting his hand move down her body again. 'Think of those little wilderness huts ... the solitude. I don't want to go without you, Jessica. We could have a second honeymoon.'

'I didn't know we'd finished our first,' she murmured, settling closer. She gasped as his hand touched a sensitive spot, moving in his arms, shifting her body so that his wandering fingers would find the spot again. 'Matt, I'd like to come——'

'So come.'

'But I can't. I've promised Mike——'

'Tell him you've changed your mind. Tell him I want you. Tell him I need you.' Matt's voice grew deeper and she struggled against her own longings. 'I do need you, Jessica.'

'I know, but——' Making a tremendous effort, she squirmed away from him and flattened her hands against his chest. 'Matt, I want to do this feature with Mike. I told you, it's important to me—to my career——'

'And that's more important than me?' Matt sat up

His tousled hair fell into his eyes and he brushed it back impatiently. Firelight glinted on his muscular body and Jessica looked away, still all too aware of his magnetism. 'Look, I thought you'd see sense——'

'After you'd made love to me, you mean?' Jessica flashed. 'You thought that once you'd proved your— your male superiority, I'd give in? You thought you only had to kiss me to make me follow you to the ends of the earth? Well, I'm sorry, Matt, but you thought wrong. Okay, so we're married, we live together, we love each other—but that doesn't give us all rights in each other. *I'm* not asking *you* to give up Finland—why should you ask me to give up my job? How am I ever going to get on, be a director, if I just tag around in your footsteps all the time? People were just beginning to take me seriously—they'll forget all about me if I go on being your P.A. and nothing else, can't you see that?'

'No, I can't. All I can see is that you've got some crackbrained idea in your head about being a director and the fact that you're married to me doesn't seem to have sunk in at all. All I can see——'

'And does being married to you mean that I can't be a director as well?' Jessica asked dangerously. 'Is wanting to be a director crackbrained just because I'm your wife, or do you really think I'm not capable of it? I'd like to know, Matt.'

'Oh, stop making mountains out of molehills,' he sneered. 'I'm only saying that a bit of ambition's all very well when you're single, but you're married now, things are different——'

'And that's just about the most chauvinistic thing I've ever heard!'

'Look, will you stop yelling at me and listen!' Matt roared, so loudly that the walls shook. Jessica jumped and stared at him; he had never shouted at her like that before. Come to that, they had never quarrelled like this before, and for a moment she wanted nothing more than to fling herself into his arms and give in. But before she could move, he was speaking again, more quietly this time. 'I just don't want you to get hurt, Jessica. Oh, it's not just the coalmine—though I'm not keen on you getting into that kind of situation, which could be dangerous. It's—well, it's the whole concept of being a director, or even a P.A. for anyone else. You know yourself, things can get pretty fraught at times. The more responsibility you have, the heavier the can is you might have to carry. I don't want you worrying about that kind of thing, Jessica. There's no need. I don't want to see you getting hurt.'

Jessica bit her lip and forced herself to lower her own voice. 'And if I want to do it? Whether I get hurt or not?'

'I don't want you to,' said Matt with a tone of finality.

'I see. And that's all there is to it. The master has spoken.' Jessica stood up and began to dress, conscious of his eyes on her body. 'I'm sorry, Matt. I've promised Mike and I don't intend to go back on that promise. I shall do the coalmine feature with him.'

'And afterwards?' Matt asked, apparently accepting her decision since it was clear she wasn't going to change it.

'I'll see.' But Jessica knew already that she wouldn't give in. It was unlikely that she would work with Matt again. She needed encouragement and help in her ambition to become a director, and it was obvious that she'd get neither of these from Matt. For those, she would have to look elsewhere.

And it was then that the first chill wind of change had touched her heart and left a tiny cold ache where previously there had been nothing but warmth.

Nothing had ever been quite the same after that, Jessica thought as she sat in her quiet cottage and stared into a fire whose light had never flickered on Matt's face or glowed on the fulfilment of their love. Oh, they'd tried—pretended. Matt hadn't tried to persuade her again to go with him to Finland, though he'd made it clear he wanted to. But he had shown as little interest as possible when she'd talked about the coalmine feature. And when she'd told him that Mike wanted her for the rest of the series, he'd just grunted and muttered something sarcastic about having to make an appointment to go to bed with her next.

Jessica had restrained herself then. But later, when Matt had discovered just what the rest of the series entailed, there'd been another confrontation, and this one hadn't ended in lovemaking.

'An *oil-rig*?' Matt exclaimed in disbelief. 'Jessica, you can't be serious! Those places are dangerous—I'm not at all sure they'll let a woman go aboard. And what's this—*Greenland*? Just what has Mike Jennings got that I haven't? You wouldn't come to Finland with me!'

'Four children for a start,' Jessica reminded him sharply. 'Don't try to make out there's something between me and Mike, Matt, because you know very well there's not. It just happens that Mike and I work well together and he teaches me a lot. And this series is the most terrific chance—I'll get experience I'd never otherwise have.'

'I don't doubt that,' Matt returned sardonically, making her want to hit him. 'Experience you couldn't have got in Finland, obviously.'

Jessica sighed. 'Don't let's go through all that again. It's getting boring. I'm doing this series with Mike, and there's not a thing you can do to stop me.'

Matt regarded her, his grey eyes veiled. 'I see,' he said eventually. 'Then there's nothing more to be said, is there? I wish you luck in your ambition, Jessica.'

There was a curious note in his voice and Jessica stared at him, conscious of a sudden stab of fear. Just what was he getting at? But before she could ask him, he had turned away and begun to talk about his own project, talking in quick, clipped tones as if to a stranger. A barrier had come down between them and there was no way she could break through it.

After that, it had been downhill all the way. Matt had

gone to Finland and was away for several weeks, during
which Jessica received only three short letters from him,
all heartbreakingly impersonal. Trying to shrug away
her fears, she immersed herself in her own work and
was rewarded by Mike's approval and congratulations;
but the core of fear, like a chip of everlasting ice, was
there in her heart whenever she relaxed her guard.

And the ice had grown when she began to hear the
rumours—rumours about Matt and the other girls. The
production assistant he had finally taken to Finland
had been a new girl, who had worked previously for a
Scottish TV station; her soft, reddish hair and lilting
voice had been an immediate attraction to all the men,
and it came as no surprise to Jessica when she heard
that Matt and Fiona had been spending a considerable
amount of time together in the Finnish forests.

'Well, he would, wouldn't he?' she'd said to the girl
who had passed on this information. 'Directors and
P.A.s do have to spend quite a bit of time together.' But
she'd said it without conviction; she and Matt had spent
time together in California and she hadn't forgotten
that last night by the river; how could she?

Afterwards, she had accepted Matt's assurances that
nothing had happened between him and Fiona. But
although their reunion had been all that she could hope
for, nothing had really changed. Her ambition to be a
director still lay between them. And the next time Matt
went away, this time to direct a drama, the rumours
had been less easy to dispel. And each time they became
more believable, until Jessica found her jealousy seeping
into every part of their life together.

It had all come to a head when Matt had gone to
America again. Not to California this time—but to
New York, where he was directing an arts documentary
on a British play which was having an unprecedented
success on the Broadway stage. And it was almost
inevitable, Jessica thought, that the rumours should
concern the leading actress in the play. And that they

should make the gossip columns of all the daily papers, so that she could no longer shrug them off or pretend that they were just the idle wagging of envious tongues. The pictures were there for all to see— pictures of Matt and Sylvia in nightclubs together, dancing close to each other, leaving arm-in-arm, smiling into each other's eyes. . . . The pictures couldn't be ignored, and as soon as Matt came home Jessica waved them in front of his face.

'All right, so I spent time with Sylvia Steele,' Matt growled. 'Do you have to believe it was anything more? I was working with her, for God's sake—the film was *about* her. I had to get to know what made her tick, didn't I?'

'Oh, that's a fine excuse,' Jessica sneered. 'Yes, of course you did. You had to dance with her, didn't you? Take her to nightclubs—stay up half the night with her. Just what else did you have to do? Just how well did you have to get to know her? Tell me that!'

'No, I'm damned if I will!' he exploded, throwing his cases down on the floor. 'My God, do I have to be interrogated like this the minute I get through the door? You know what you have to do if you want to keep an eye on me, Jessica—come with me! That's if you're so mistrustful that you think I need keeping an eye on. Or perhaps you'd rather employ a private eye to follow me wherever I go?'

'I'd rather not have to do either——' Jessica began, tightlipped, and he interrupted her with a harsh laugh.

'Then don't!'

'But what *am* I to believe—when I see things like this?' She looked up at him, her hazel eyes huge and blurred with tears. 'And it isn't just this time—it's *all* the time now. If it's not an actress it's your P.A., and if it's not her it's the make-up girl. How can I be sure?'

'That's up to you.' Matt turned away and picked up his cases. His face was set and cold. 'You could just try trusting me. You know what this business is like—it thrives on rumours and gossip. If you can't take it—well, you'll just have to do something else.'

'Like what?' Jessica stood with the newspapers in her hand, staring at him, aware that they had come to a kind of crossroads and that the next few moments were going to be vital to them both.

'Like making up your mind just what you want to do. About us—about our life together. Because if you ask me, neither of us is getting much out of it at present.' Matt started to go upstairs, then turned and looked down at her. He was immense, seen from below with the shadow cast by the hall light looming behind him—immense, and dark, and threatening. 'If it gives you any satisfaction, Jessica, I'm not going to deny those rumours about me and Sylvia Steele. I'm not going to deny anything you care to accuse me with—there doesn't seem to be much point. Believe what you like—and do what you like about it. But just don't disturb me for the next twelve hours or so, right? I've had a heavy trip and I just want to sleep.'

By the time he woke, Jessica had gone. Dazed and only half aware of what she was doing, she'd collected together as much as she needed for a couple of weeks and left the house. She'd been due for some time off—had even hoped that she and Matt might spend it together, perhaps even on that holiday in Finland—and she went to Cornwall, telling nobody where she was going, spending her days walking on the cliffs or the beach and her nights in the anonymous bed of a seaside hotel.

When she returned to the house she and Matt had shared, it was empty. Only her belongings were left, together with the furniture. And Jessica, staring around the unwelcoming rooms in increasing dismay, knew that she had come to the end of that particular road. She hadn't, as she returned, been at all sure of what she had expected. Subconsciously, she supposed she had still been hoping for a reconciliation. It was clear now that there was no such hope.

She had run out on Matt, and that was something he wasn't prepared to take.

It was late when Jessica finally went to bed. As she undressed, she looked around the bedroom. Nobody had ever shared it with her; since she had left Matt—or he had left her, she was never sure which it was—there had been no other man in her life. Bruised by her short and storm-ridden marriage, she had withdrawn emotionally, determined not to risk being hurt again. All her energies and frustrations had been sublimated in her work, and she had been rewarded at last by her promotion to director. Now she had achieved sufficient recognition to go freelance, able to pick and choose. That, at least, was something to show Matt—some proof that she'd been right to set her own goal.

And she had to admit that he had acknowledged that—otherwise he would never have given her this job. Did that mean he was ready to think again—to pick up the threads of their marriage?

No! Whatever he felt, that wasn't what Jessica had in mind, no way! She hadn't come this far to give in to him. For she was under no illusion—if Matt and she resumed their marriage, it would be with the same problems, the same contentions. They had each moved up a step, Matt to producer, she to director, but the situation would remain the same. Matt would still consider her job unimportant, her function to be his wife. And Jessica wasn't prepared to go along with that. Success hadn't come easily enough for her to throw it away at his behest.

So what was she going to do, once this film was over? She lay awake, one lamp burning low, gazing at the sloping ceiling, the tiny flowers on the wallpaper. Could she possibly go on working at Mercia TV if Matt were to be a permanent member of the staff? Wouldn't it be better to get out, before they could get involved all over again? Move right away—even go abroad?

She thought of Chantal Gordon. There had been something peculiarly possessive in the older woman's attitude towards Matt. As if their relationship were a good deal more intimate than that of producer and subject. Well, that wouldn't be surprising. In fact, remembering the anthropologist's sophisticated beauty, she would have been surprised if Matt hadn't started some kind of relationship. But there had been something Chantal had said—what was it?—something about the 'magic five'.

Jessica hadn't taken a lot of notice at the time. But now it struck home. She and Matt had been separated for over four years—she'd told Chantal that herself. After five years, either of them could divorce the other without consent; with a good deal less trouble.

Was that what Matt had in mind? Jessica stared miserably at the pretty wallpaper. She had, during the past four years, occasionally thought of divorce, but had never been able to bring herself to do anything about it. Presumably the same had applied to Matt; he had sold the house some months after they had parted and sent her half the money, but apart from that she had demanded nothing from him and they had had no contact. Unless either of them wanted to remarry divorce had seemed just another painful procedure which could be avoided.

But perhaps Chantal, who no doubt knew a good deal more about Matt's present frame of mind than Jessica did, was aware of Matt's plans. Perhaps she was even involved in them. Would Matt have discussed his marriage and a possible divorce with her if he had not expected her to be closely interested—if, Jessica put it baldly to herself, he didn't want Chantal Gordon to become Chantal Fenwood?

It doesn't mean a thing to you, not a thing, she scolded herself fiercely. You haven't considered yourself married to Matt for four years now. It's the only sensible thing, to get a divorce and cut the ties cleanly and finally away. And if Matt wants to get married again, good luck to him—and even better luck to her! For Jessica had her own first-hand experience of trying to be married to Matt and keep her own career going. Chantal would need a good deal of luck on her side if she were to try it too. Unless Matt had changed radically in the meantime.

Determined to forget the whole business, she snapped off her light and settled down to sleep. But it was a long time before sleep came; and when it did she dreamed of being with Matt again, making love in their old abandoned way. And when she woke in the morning her head ached, and her pillow was wet with tears.

CHAPTER FIVE

JESSICA was working late one evening, papers spread out before her on her living-room table as she tried to shape some kind of sequence for her film, when the telephone rang. Still looking thoughtfully at her plans, she answered absently, and was pleasantly surprised to hear Chris's voice.

'Hullo, Jessica. Just thought you'd like to know, I've found a derelict cottage.'

'You have? That's wonderful! Will we be able to use it, do you think?'

'Yes, I've talked with the local authority and they seem to think it'll be okay. They'd just passed it for demolition anyway. Pity, really—it's in a delightful situation, as the estate agents say. But right off the beaten track—up a really rough old road that hasn't been maintained for about a hundred years, from the state of it.'

'That's good. We won't be causing too much local disturbance.'

'No, and I can't imagine too many letters of complaint to the local papers. Especially after people have seen us doing it up only to set fire to it—I can just see that being a real bone of contention.'

'Will it need much doing up?' asked Jessica, thinking of the budget. She was prepared to do anything necessary, but was still uncomfortably aware that what Chris had said was true—this was going to be an expensive project.

'Not a lot. It's the inside that's falling to bits. It could actually be restored, in my opinion, but nobody wants to live there—not even your rich Midlands business-man!'

'Well, that's fine. And what about the good cottage—the one we'll be using for interiors? Any luck in that direction?'

'Not concrete, though I'm hoping. Emlyn gave me a name—friend of his, retired architect who bought a cottage on the Mawdacch Estuary just above Barmouth. It looks right out over the water towards Cader Idris—not far from Emlyn's. He says it's been restored beautifully on the inside, has a big picture window overlooking the estuary both in the living-room and upstairs in the main bedroom. The rooms are fairly big, too—been knocked together at some stage, I imagine.'

'That sounds ideal. Some of these cottages are so tiny we'd never get the actors in along with the cameras and lights and everything! Are you going to see it?'

'Tomorrow,' Chris told her triumphantly. 'I spoke to the owner on the phone today and he sounds a very pleasant, affable chap—invited me along to lunch. His wife's an artist.'

'Well, that all sounds fine. I wonder if I ought to come along too. I'll have to see the place.'

'That's why I rang now. The invitation's for you as well—I told him you'd need to see it and talk to him about it. I wasn't sure if you'd be able to make it, though.'

'Oh yes, I'll make it.' Jessica gathered her papers up with one hand. 'I'll drive straight over and see you there. Just give me the details. I come the same way as we went to Emlyn's, don't I?'

Quickly she jotted down the details Chris gave her, and then put down the phone. Chris had done well, she thought, going into the kitchen to make a hot drink. Things were really beginning to move at last.

But there was still a great deal to arrange before they could begin filming. And for some reason it was desperately important to her that they finish before Matt returned to England. This was something she had to do without his interference.

It was a clear and sparkling spring day when Jessica arrived at the top of the hill leading down into the little Welsh seaside town of Barmouth next morning. Following Chris's directions, she went down a narrow path at the side of a tall house and found herself at the side of a white-painted cottage, hidden from the road and looking out across the wide estuary. For a few moments she stood there staring at the view.

It would, she thought, have been difficult to imagine a more beautiful one. Below the cottage, the cliff dropped steeply away from a terraced garden to the sands beneath; sands that would, in a few hours, be covered by the high tide. The river at present was little more than a narrow stream, winding its way between the yellow sandbanks to the sea, but as the tide came in the entire stretch between here and the far bank—not far short of a mile, she guessed—would become a huge blue lake, with the height of Cader Idris an emerald backcloth topped by brown crags. Then it would become a playground for sailors, with dinghies and cruisers making bright spots of colour on the rippling water. Now, it was a feeding-ground for a vast number of wading birds—oyster-catchers with their handsome black and white plumage and long orange bills, sandpipers, redshanks and the long-legged curlews whose bubbling cry she could hear as she stood there. If they used this cottage, they would just have to include a shot of this marvellous view.

Jessica turned along the low wall and found a gate. It led her to a patio above the terraced garden, and as she passed in front of the big window she saw the occupants of the cottage get up to welcome her at the door.

'You must be Mrs Fenwood. Come in, come in. You've brought a beautiful day with you.'

'It's lovely, isn't it? And what a beautiful spot—I was just admiring the view.' Jessica slipped off her jacket and followed her host into the living-room. It was just as Chris had said it would be, large and light, with the window framing its view like a picture. It was a homely room, comfortable and pleasantly furnished; the fireplace wall was of rough stone but the other walls were panelled with stripped pine and hung with pictures or lined with bookshelves. A chintz-covered sofa and chairs stood around the room, and in the window bay were two matching benches with soft cushions. On the hearth stood a tall basket filled with logs and near it was a low table with a Welsh pottery coffee jug and a set of mugs on it.

Jessica sat down in the window, accepted a mug of coffee, and began to chat to the Hartes, whom she soon discovered to be as affable as Chris had said. George Harte was a round-faced man with twinkling blue eyes and a ready smile; he had the attractive habit of seeming immediately interested in everything Jessica had to say, and asked a good many questions about the film, showing himself to be intelligent enough to understand her answers with very little explanation. His wife, Ann, was a small woman with an equally round but pretty face, framed in curling grey hair; she listened quietly for the most part but had her own questions too, and it was clear that they were both intrigued by the idea of having their cottage used as a location for filming, as well as approving wholeheartedly of the subject.

'It's a silly position ever to have got into, this Welsh cottage business,' George Harte declared. 'There should have been some kind of restriction—a price barrier, perhaps—to prevent its ever arising. Easy to say, of course—it would have been almost impossible to enforce. But the whole thing is a vicious circle.'

'That's exactly what I'm setting out to show,' Jessica agreed eagerly. 'And Emlyn's book is going to be splendid in illustrating it. You've read it, I suppose?'

'Oh yes. I've often wondered why it hasn't been televised. Perhaps after this it will be—as a follow-up.'

'Yes, that's quite an idea,' Jessica said thoughtfully. 'I

wonder if it could be arranged. It may be too late, of course— and we'd have to get a script ready and book the same actors. I might mention it to the producer, though.'

At those words, her mind jerked and she remembered that Matt was the producer. For just a little while she'd almost forgotten! Ruefully, she wished that she could forget more often, and then jumped up as Ann Harte offered to show her the rest of the cottage.

'It really is lovely,' she said, following the other woman from the room. 'And you've got that spectacular view from every window! How often have you painted it? Chris told me you were an artist.'

'Oh yes, it's a blessing, that view,' said Ann Harte, leading the way upstairs. 'I think I've painted it in all its moods. I hardly know which I like best—when it's clear and sunny, like today, or when it's dark and threatening, as it can be all too often. We've seen some very exciting thunderstorms from our windows.'

The bedroom was light, with a small balcony just outside the big patio window. Ann Harte showed Jessica the little breakfast bar and fridge that her husband had built into one wall, and told her that they often had breakfast on the balcony on fine mornings. 'It's sheltered, even though it looks out on the estuary,' she explained. 'And if we have guests they can use the kitchen downstairs so that we all meet later, when we feel more civilised!'

'I think it's all highly civilised,' Jessica smiled. 'And I'd really like to use it for the film, if you're happy with the idea. It means a certain amount of upheaval, I'm afraid—but I wouldn't expect to be here for more than two or three days, and the crew are always very careful.'

'That's fine—just let us know when you want to come.' Ann led the way back down the stairs. There were paintings everywhere, Jessica noticed, and she paused to look at some of them. They were mostly watercolours, with a few oils and sketches, and she could see that they had all been executed by the same hand. Ann Harte's neat signature was in the bottom right-hand corner of each one.

'These are lovely—you've really caught the spirit of the place,' she began, bending to look at a group showing the view across the estuary in all its moods. 'Oh, and I know where this is, it's——' And then she stopped abruptly. Her heart gave a great lurch and then seemed to stop completely. And all her pleasure in the morning seemed to drain out through the soles of her feet and through the solid stone floor.

'Which one's that?' Ann Harte had turned and was beside her, looking to see what had caught her eye. As she glanced at Jessica, her face changed and she put out an arm quickly.

'My dear, what's the matter? Are you all right? You've gone as white as a sheet.'

'I'm ... all right,' Jessica mumbled, but she swayed and Ann caught her sleeve and guided her to a chair.

'Sit down. Put your head down—you'll feel better in a moment.' She held Jessica until sure she wasn't going to faint, then called her husband. 'George! Bring Jessica some water, will you? She's feeling a little queasy.' She fed Jessica the water in little sips, while George hovered anxiously in the background. 'There. Feeling better now?'

'Yes, thank you.' Jessica raised her head. 'I'm sorry—I don't know what came over me. I'll be fine now.'

'Can you walk into the living-room? That's right—now, rest on this sofa for a while.' Ann gazed at her anxiously. 'Are you really feeling better?'

'Yes, honestly. It must have been bending down like that—I just felt a bit dizzy for a minute, that's all.' Jessica looked up, mustering the brightest smile she could manage. 'I'll be quite all right, don't worry.'

'Well, perhaps if we leave you in peace for a few minutes.' Ann looked half-convinced as she turned to go. 'There are a few things I need to do in the kitchen, and I can see a young man coming along the side—I expect that's your colleague. George can show him round while you rest. Now, you're sure you're feeling better?'

'Yes, quite sure,' Jessica assured her, and the Hartes left the room. Almost at once, she heard Chris's voice outside, answered by George's more measured tones, and then the voices faded and she could hear only the small sounds Ann made as she worked in the kitchen.

Jessica closed her eyes and leaned back. She'd spoken truthfully when she told Ann Harte that she felt better—that first wave of nauseating dizziness had left her. But she still felt shaken and in need of a few moments' solitude to regain her equilibrium. And she had lied when she attributed her faintness to bending to look at the pictures. It had a far more potent cause than that.

It hadn't been the little group of paintings of the estuary that had caught her eye then, but the more vibrant colours of gold, brown and orange of a garden full of flowers; the clear yellow of a cluster of huge sunflowers with their chocolate-coloured seedheads, the orange of nasturtiums, a riot of almost harsh colour by the banks of a river. And above, towering into the clear sky, old and decaying and unmistakable, a French château.

Jessica knew that château. She had seen it every morning when she woke, looming high above as she leaned out of her window opposite and sniffed the fresh morning air. She had seen it by moonlight, glimmering in the silvered shadows, and she had wondered about its history, imagining the barons who had built it, a fortress from which they could control their estates; their aristocratic descendants, rich, decadent and uncaring before they were toppled and driven away. But she had not really had very much time to think about the château. She'd been on her honeymoon, after all, and as eager as Matt to discover the delights of today.

She still had, at home, a box which contained pictures of that château—photographs she had taken, showing Matt relaxed and happy, photographs he had taken of her, ecstatic and content. Their rented cottage in the background and, towering over it, the turrets of the château. She must have seen the garden that Ann Harte had painted, must have passed it on her way to the village for rolls and cheese and *pâté*. She wondered when the Hartes had been there, but knew she would never ask them. A discussion on the tiny French village and its delights would bring it all back so much more painfully, and she knew that she couldn't face it.

No. Better to forget. Forget the picture; forget the memories; forget—if she could ever forget—Matt.

The door opened quietly and Jessica turned her head, expecting to see Ann Harte. But it was Chris who came in, his face full of concern. Before she could speak, he was beside her, his blue eyes searching hers anxiously.

'Jessica, are you all right? Mrs Harte told me you'd felt faint—you're not ill, are you?'

'No, I'm fine, honestly. Just felt a bit woozy for a minute—the long drive, I expect, and I didn't have much breakfast. There's nothing to worry about, Chris.'

'Well, I'm glad to hear it,' he said a little more lightly. 'Can't have our director cracking up! You do look a bit washed-out, though, Jessica. It isn't too much for you, is it, this film?'

'No, of course it's not!' she snapped, then relented as she saw Chris's expression. 'Oh, I'm sorry, Chris. Only it's just the kind of thing that would absolutely delight Matt—if I couldn't cope with this. And I'm just not going to give him the opportunity to say "I told you so"—he always sneered at my wanting to direct. I know I can make a good job of this, and I intend to.' Suddenly aware that she was still half-lying on the sofa, she swung her feet to the floor, flicking her long auburn hair back from her face.

Chris pursed his lips. 'I'm not sure you're right there,' he said judiciously. 'About Matt, I mean. He may not have had much faith in you once, but surely he must have now, or he wouldn't have given you this job. You don't seriously think he wants you to fail, do you?'

'Yes! Well—no, perhaps not. That wouldn't do *his* reputation much good, after all. And Matt's reputation means a lot to him.' Jessica sighed. 'Oh, perhaps you're right, Chris. I'm overreacting. I just wish it was anyone but Matt producing. Even though he's in Africa I can feel his eyes on me, with that awful, critical in-a-minute-she'll-do-something-stupid look in them, just as he used to look when I was driving or doing anything else that he thought was his province!'

Chris laughed. 'Being a typical husband, in fact! I didn't know we had so much influence! But you're not going to do anything stupid, Jessica. I'm as sure as you are that this is going to be a fantastic film.'

Jessica looked up at him. 'Thank you, Chris,' she said quietly, and their eyes met and held; blue with hazel, sky with the greenish-gold of a summer hillside. Jessica felt her heart quicken suddenly, then she looked away and the moment passed. She got up and went to the window, remarking on the beautiful view.

'You've really struck oil here, Chris,' she said as he came to stand beside her. 'It couldn't be better for filming. It's got everything. Look—the tide's coming in.'

'Yes, and it comes in pretty quickly here, too.' They watched as the water spread rapidly over the flat sands, filling the channels cut by the river and overflowing to make rapidly-diminishing yellow islands on which the birds still gathered, picking up what food they could in the knowledge that this larder would be closed to them for several hours now. A train chugged its way across the long bridge below and already a few fishermen were arriving, ready to catch what they could. Somewhere on the far bank the sun glinted on the windscreen of a car.

'It all looks so peaceful,' Jessica remarked, turning away. 'One can't imagine people getting so angry that they'd burn down other people's houses. This one, for instance—could anyone ever do it to this lovely place?'

Chris shrugged. 'I suppose they could, though as you say it hardly seems possible. But in the right circumstances. . . . It will make a wonderful contrast, Jessica.'

'Yes. We must show Huw very carefully when he comes to set fire to it—show just how much he really loves the place, how he feels he's been robbed of what should have been his home. It makes his actions all the more poignant—he's doing it out of desperation as much as resentment. He's completely confused, doesn't know how to retrieve all the things he's lost—his home, his job, his marriage, the baby that died. And of course, most of them he *can't* retrieve. They're gone for ever and he's got to start from scratch, but he can't at the moment see that there'll ever be anything else worth having. So when he sets fire to the cottage he doesn't do it with any real hope that it will make things better in any way; he's just trying to express what he feels about what's happened to him.'

They continued to discuss the film over lunch; the Hartes were both genuinely interested and their conversation gave Jessica several fresh ideas and new dimensions on the points of view she was trying to illuminate. Afterwards, she and Chris had another look round, considering where they could get effective shots, then Jessica thanked the Hartes and told them she would be in touch as soon as she had some firm dates.

'I'll have to bring the camera crew for a recce,' she said, 'but that won't take long. And I should think we'll need to be here for two or three days. We'll say three at this stage, to be safe. Is there any time that wouldn't be convenient—are you likely to be away at all in the next month or so?'

'Not that we know of,' said George Harte, 'but we'll let you know at once if anything crops up. Well, it's all very interesting, Jessica. We'll look forward to seeing the filming—it'll be quite a new experience for us.'

'I thought we'd call in on Emlyn Thomas on the way back,' Chris suggested as they made their way back to their cars. 'I gave him a ring yesterday and he said he'd be in. I think he's got some news for you.'

'News?' But Chris only grinned and refused to say any more, and Jessica, following him in her car, was left to wonder what it might be.

Well, she thought as they drove along the road that led beside the river into the mountains, at least wondering about that kept her mind off Matt. And just what he might be doing at this very moment under the hot African sun. Or was it—she was never any good at time-zones—now night there, and whatever he was doing taking place under the velvety canopy of an African night, lit only by the needle-points of a myriad stars. . . .

By the time Jessica had left Emlyn Thomas's house, high up in the green hills, her mind was at last too excitedly busy to think about Matt. The 'news' that Emlyn had given her was enough to drive all thoughts of her marriage completely out of her head, and for the first time Matt's shadow and the sensation that his eyes were on her had thoughts vanished, leaving her free to think and plan without the subconscious fear of his disapproval that had haunted her all along.

As she drove back to Shrewsbury through a deepening twilight, she thought of the difference this would make to the film. The dramatised sequences would become reality, highlighting events that had really taken place. Viewers would hear in his own words, his own voice, just why 'Huw' had taken the drastic action of firing a cottage he had wanted for his home. And if he talked on soundtrack and film as he'd talked to her that afternoon, he couldn't fail to move them.

She thought of her arrival at the old farmhouse that afternoon; Emlyn's welcome, Mair's smiling face. Chris had evidently been in on the secret, but Emlyn, with an endearing childlike delight in springing surprise, had made him promise not to tell her. So when she had first walked into the living-room and found the thin young man, awkward and lanky with a lock of dark hair falling over his forehead, she hadn't immediately understood.

'Jessica,' Emlyn had said, coming into the room behind her, 'this is a young man I think you'll be pleased to meet. His name's Euan Parry.' He watched her face for a moment, holding the suspense as long as he could, then added quietly: 'Better known to you, perhaps as Huw.'

'Huw?' Jessica repeated, still not understanding, then: '*Huw?* You—you mean *our* Huw? Your Huw? The Huw in your book?'

'That's it, girl.' Emlyn was clearly enjoying her blaze of excitement. 'Huw himself. He's agreed to talk to you. Whether you'll get him to go on film is another matter, of course.'

Jessica turned wonderingly to the young man. Here he was, before her in the flesh, the young man whose story had moved Emlyn Thomas to write a book about him. It wasn't a straight biography—Emlyn had added ideas of his own—but the basic tragedy was the same; the story of a young couple, driven from their home surroundings to live and work in the alien environment of a big city, with the strains and stresses inevitably resulting from the enforced move bringing about their own sad consequences. And this was the young man at the centre of that story; thin to the point of gauntness, with hollowed eyes and a pale, nervy face.

Jessica held out her hand and Euan Parry took it after a moment's hesitation. He hadn't dressed up for this meeting, she thought, noting his worn denims and washed-out T-shirt. Perhaps he had nothing to dress up in. But the wariness in his eyes told her that although he had agreed to this meething, he might still be a very long way from agreeing to anything else—such as appearing in her film.

Jessica knew that she must now call up all her powers of tack and persuasion. Euan Parry was like a shy wld animal; one false move and he would be away. She must gain his confidence before she even hinted at what she really wanted.

And as she drove home that evening, following the red lights of Chris's car ahead, she felt a sense of satisfaction and certainty that she had done just that. As they talked together through the afternoon she had seen Euan's manner change from wary suspicion to a gradual acceptance of her. Almost tonguetied at first, he had slowly thawed, answering her gentle questions to begin with by monosyllables, but eventually speaking at greater length even though he was still hesitant and obviously unused to putting his feelings into words. But that made it all the more moving, she thought, recalling the way he had glanced at Emlyn for support and realising just how much Emlyn must have gained his confidence while he was researching for his book. And it couldn't have been easy for him to persuade Euan to see her this afternoon; Jessica had received the strong impression that Euan was there much against his own convictions and had only come to please the older man.

But he *had* come, and he'd promised to see her again. He hadn't, as she'd guessed, been keen on the idea of appearing on film, even in dim lighting with his back to the camera, which wasn't one of Jessica's favourite devices anyway. But he hadn't turned down the possibility of his voice being used on wildtrack—recorded in sound only so that it could be used as a voice-over during the film. Perhaps during a silent part of the dramatisation, Jessica thought, while Huw was being shown creeping around the cottage and setting fire to it. Euan's voice then, telling the true story of his own feelings, would be both moving and dramatic, and Jessica felt her heart give a bump of excitement as she visualised it.

By the time she reached her cottage the sky was quite dark and stars had begun to appear. She put the car away in the little garage and stood by the door for a moment, breathing in the hot scent of wallflowers and listening to the hooting of a pair of owls in the wood nearby. There were no other sounds; the cottage was far enough away from the main road, down its quiet lane, for the noise of traffic to be muted, and in any case there was little on that particular road at night.

Jessica gave a little sigh of contentment. She loved her cottage and had begun at last to put down roots. For a long time, she had been afraid to do that; the break-up of her marriage had left her bruised and unsure of herself, afraid to trust in anything again. But now—now she was free. Or could be, soon—completely free. She'd made her own way, proved herself, she had her own home. And if an Englishman's home was his castle, didn't that apply to an Englishwoman too? Wasn't even a tiny cottage, like this one, just as good a fortress as the Tower of London, if you wanted it to be?

Jessica took one last look round, then felt in her pocket for the key. She was just fitting it into the lock when the telephone rang. She was standing in the open doorway, still in darkness and looking out at the stars when she answered it and heard Matt's voice, like a shock hitting her heart, shattering her peace.

'Jessica? And how's my lovely wife tonight? It *is* night, isn't it?'

Dry-mouthed, Jessica could only nod and whisper her answer, before his repeated question; then, gathering her strength together, she croaked, 'Yes. Yes, it's about eight o'clock. Matt, what——'

'Just thought I'd like a little chat,' he cut in cheerfully. 'Seems a long time since we said goodbye. How's it going, Jessica?'

'How's what going? The film?' Indignation came to her rescue. So this was how much he trusted her—telephoning all the way from Africa to check up! 'Why don't you ring Graham and ask him? He seems fairly satisfied.'

'Oh, I'm sure everything's fine.' His voice came back smoothly after the tiny hesitation due to the distance. 'I wasn't really asking about the film.'

'So what *are* you ringing about?'

She could almost see Matt's shrug at the other end. 'Just to see how you were. Just to say hallo. Just——' his voice was very low now, as soft as velvet '—just to hear your voice.'

Completely nonplussed, Jessica stared mutely out of the door. To hear her voice? What nonsense was he talking? Until recently, he hadn't heard her voice for four years—he'd never bothered then to ring her up, even from London. So why should he do it now? Especially when he had Chantal to occupy his mind.

'Jessica? Are you still there?'

'Yes, I'm still here,' she said dully, knowing that the most sensible thing would be to put down the phone, but somehow unable to do so.

'Tell me something,' he said coaxingly. 'Tell me what it's like where you are. Is it raining or dry? Warm or cold? Tell me——'

'Matt!' she expostulated. 'You didn't ring me up to talk about the *weather*!'

'Why not? I told you, I just wanted to hear your voice. You can read me the telephone directory if you like. I don't mind. But why don't you just tell me what sort of evening it is?'

'Because I—oh, all right.' She glanced out of the open door. 'Well, it's dark. There's just been a lovely sunset and the air's very soft and warm, more like early

June than April. I can smell the wall-flowers and there's
a tawny owl somewhere in the wood. I think there's a
pair nesting there. There are tits nesting in the garden
too, in the boxes I put up last year. Great tits and
bluetits. And a robin, in an old kettle in the hedge.' She
stopped suddenly, wondering what had possessed her to
talk to Matt like this. It must be standing here in the
dark, looking out at the friendly evening. 'Well, is that
what you wanted?' she asked sharply.

'Just what I wanted.' Matt's voice was more than
ever like rich brown velvet. 'And don't I wish I were
there to share it with you? Remember the cottage in
France, Jessica? Where we spent our honeymoon?
There were evenings like that there, weren't there? Soft
and warm, as soft and warm as you were in my arms,
and as made for loving. Remember them, Jessica? But
of course you do. How could you forget?'

Jessica trembled so violently that her legs refused to
hold her and she sank down to the floor, leaning
against the wall and clutching the receiver tightly. What
was happening? Why should Matt telephone her all the
way from Africa and remind her of their honeymoon,
when she had only that day been reminded of it once
already? Had something communicated itself to him
from her troubled thoughts? She'd always been aware
of his almost uncanny ability to sense what was in her
mind—but that was when they were together, not
thousands of miles apart! Was she never going to be
safe from his seeking eyes, even when there was a world
between them?

'Remember those nights, Jessica?' Matt was continu-
ing. 'The whole world belonged to us then, didn't it?
We didn't need anyone else, did we? And it was't just
the nights was it? Remember the days—those long, hot
days when we took a boat down the river and found a
secluded bank where we could swim and sunbathe?
You'd never swum in the nude before, had you—I
remember your delicious shyness. But it didn't last too

long, did it—remember? I'd never made love to a real live mermaid before . . . under a Gallic sun. I never have since.'

'You have my sympathy,' Jessica said, her voice shaking in spite of her efforts to speak coldly. 'Matt, if you don't mind——'

'And that day we walked in the forest,' he mused, ignoring her interruption. 'Under those tall, cool trees. Remember the scent of the pine-needles as we crushed them beneath our bodies, Jessica? Wasn't it the experience of a lifetime? Wasn't it an experience you'd like to repeat?'

Jessica shivered. Try as she would, she couldn't prevent Matt's words recalling images to her mind— images of the two of them sunbathing and swimming naked together, making love on the grassy banks under the hot sun; lying entwined beneath the towering pines, the air heavy with the sharp scent of resin. Waves of heat swept over her body and she could feel the responsive swelling of her breasts, the tingling low in her stomach. She wanted to put the phone down, stop listening, knew that she should if she were to sleep at all that night; but Matt's voice was compulsive and she held it close against her ear. Ann Harte's picture of the French château came into her mind and she closed her eyes, almost able to see the crumbling stonework, almost able to smell the flowers in the hot evening air.

'Perhaps we'll go back again some time,' Matt was murmuring now. 'Do it all again—recapture those times. Or don't you believe in going back, Jessica? Do you think it's better to go on, looking ahead all the time, progressing?' He paused and then added in a tone so low she barely heard it: 'What do you want to progress to, Jessica?'

Jessica found her voice at last. 'I don't want to progress to anything with you, Matt,' she said, wishing that her voice would sound firmer. 'I thought we both

understood that. Look—I don't know what the purpose
of this call is, but I've only just got in and——'

'Don't you?' he cut in. 'Don't you know, really? Stop
fooling yourself, Jessica. Because you're fooling no one
else, you know. Least of all me.'

There was a tiny silence. Then Jessica said in a dry
voice: 'Just what do you mean, Matt?'

'Maybe I won't tell you that now,' he said
thoughtfully. 'Maybe it will be better kept. But you
think about it, Jessica, when you go to your lonely bed.
Think about what I've said; think about those nights
and days in France; think about what you threw away.
And then ask yourself who you're fooling. Will you do
that?'

'And if I do,' Jessica said tightly, 'what will you be
thinking about—in your lonely bed? Or maybe it isn't
quite so lonely.' She let a few seconds tick by and then
added casually: 'And how *is* Chantal?'

There was the tiniest of pauses, little more than a
heartbeat of time, and then Matt said harshly, his voice
completely changed: 'I'll say goodnight now, Jessica.
Sleep well—if you can.' And she heard the click as a
telephone receiver was replaced somewhere in Africa.

If I can, she thought bitterly as she climbed stiffly to
her feet and replaced her own instrument. And just
what hope is there for that? She closed the door on the
night and switched on the lamp. All her excitement in
the day had evaporated and she felt flattened, deflated,
dull. The sexual excitement that Matt had awoken in
her had died away to an uncomfortable frustration.
Why had he done it? she wondered bitterly as she moved
towards the kitchen. To torment her? A belated
punishment for what she'd done to him four years
earlier, when she'd left him? A reminder that he could
still, at the flick of a dial, control both her emotions
and her life?

As she had closed the door, she'd picked up the daily
newspaper from the floor. She dropped it on the

kitchen table as she took the kettle to the tap. A cup of coffee might help, and perhaps she ought to make some sort of a meal—though she didn't feel like eating a thing. But it was a long time since Mair Thomas's Welsh tea, ample though that had been.

Scrambled eggs—she might be able to manage that. It was important to keep going, behave normally. Matt would be delighted to know that his effect on her had been so drastic—and though he couldn't really know either way, his uncomfortable and almost telephathic powers of awareness made her feel that she must put on a bold front even when she was quite alone. And if the phone rang again—well, she just wouldn't answer it.

But why had he reacted like that to her enquiry about Chantal Gordon? All right, her meaning had been clear enough—she'd intended it to be. She'd wanted him to know that he couldn't pull the wool over her eyes in that particular way any more. But she didn't see why he should take exception to that. It had been true often enough before, hadn't it? Why shouldn't it be true this time? And if it wasn't—well, Matt had only himself to blame for his reputation, hadn't he?

Jessica took eggs from the fridge and cracked them into a bowl. She put a knob of butter into a small pan and melted it, then beat the eggs into it and made toast in the toaster. She made coffee while the eggs were setting, then stirred them vigorously and tipped the creamy mass over the toast. She did the whole thing quite mechanically and hardly noticed her own actions.

Then she sat down at the kitchen table and drew the newspaper towards her, eating automatically as she turned the pages.

The news stories floated before her eyes, all seeming oddly familiar. A strike somewhere in a car factory; a baby lost; a fire in a foreign hotel; quins born to a woman who had been treated for infertility. On the gossip page, a story about the Royal Family and a picture of some actress out with her latest escort.

And, right at the bottom, a story about Matt Fenwood and Chantal Gordon.

Jessica stared stupidly at it. She didn't take it in at all at first. Matt's face looked out at her from the page, smudged with bad printing but still recognisable, his expression grim. Chantal was smiling, though, teeth dazzling in an obviously suntanned face, hair sleek and shining, low-cut blouse just showing the curve of her breasts. Her arm was linked in Matt's and her head drooped invitingly towards his shoulder.

The story was quite brief. Headed 'Is this Chantal's Tarzan?' it told, in a suitably double-edged manner, that Matt and Chantal were working on a film of new excavations in Africa. It also made it quite clear that excavations were not all that they were working on, and speculated openly that Matt Fenwood might be the right man at last for the beautiful Miss Gordon, who had already been married once and engaged three times.

It did not mention Jessica. Which was, she thought as she stared at it and felt her senses slowly return from the numbnesss, some comfort at least.

Picking the paper up, she read through the story again and looked more closely at the picture. Matt certainly looked grim—but then he never had liked being photographed. Chantal, on the other hand, clearly loved it. Her smile was that of the cat who has permanent access to the cream, and the way her arm was linked with Matt's was nothing short of possessive.

So why had Matt rung her that evening? Why had he talked that way, reminding her of their honeymoon, making her respond to him even when he was thousands of miles away?

Was it because he knew about the gossip item and knew that she would have seen it? And if so, was his call intended as a reassurance—or was it something else? A refined form of torture, perhaps—a deliberate awakening of her senses so that he could have the sadistic pleasure of slapping them down?

Just what was Matt Fenwood trying to do to her?

CHAPTER SIX

MATT didn't ring again, and Jessica roamed about the
cottage in the evenings unsure whether to be relieved or
disappointed. She had given up all hope of being able to
push him out of her mind; his telephone call had slipped
in under her guard and the gossip item had given her
seesawing emotions a violent swing so that she no
longer knew what she thought or felt. Her only
coherent wish was that Matt had kept away from her.
In only a few months he could have divorced her
without even making contact; why, oh, why couldn't he
have done just that? What was the point of this
harassment? What was he hoping to achieve?

She did, however, manage to regain her excitement
over the film, and had now made out a fairly
comprehensive plan of action. The casting director had
arranged for several actors and actresses to meet her in
London the following week, and Jessica had confirmed
the date of the weeks she had booked the film crew.
There was still a great deal to arrange: documentary
sequences and interviews, other locations to be used for
both the documentary and dramatisation, the superficial
renovation of the derelict cottage—not amounting to
much more than a lick of paint on the window-frames
and a few slates on the roof, to her relief—and the co-
ordination of the services which would be needed for
the actual fire scene. Police, fire and ambulance services
all had to be notified and payments arranged for those
who actually attended. Jessica also found it necessary to
contact experts at the studios who would advise her on
the management of the fire itself, and arrange for them
to be present at the shooting. As well as all this, she
discussed with Emlyn the appearance and dress of the

102

characters in the drama sequences and talked with the wardrobe section.

All this took time and thought, and there were constantly small points cropping up which hadn't been considered. Chris and Hilary, the production assistant, both helped a great deal, but the burden of each decision rested finally on Jessica's shoulders and it wasn't surprising that, by the time she set off for London the following week to cast the drama, she was feeling rather tired.

It was, she found rather pleasant to be in London for a couple of days—almost like being on holiday. She walked quickly through the thronged streets, noticing all over again the number of foreign faces—some holidaymakers and tourists, others clearly residents. A foreign face was rare in Shrewsbury, where few immigrants apart from the owners of the local Chinese restaurant had penetrated, and each time she came to London she noticed it afresh. The whole atmosphere was different, too; a concentrated bustle, contrasting sharply with the more leisurely way of life in Shrewsbury's ancient roads and passages between the timbered buildings.

Today she was to see the people the casting director had thought might be suitable for the parts of the young couple, Huw and Olwen. She wondered if any of them might actually look like the real-life Huw, and hoped not. The temptation to choose him might be too great, yet he might not prove to be the best choice and any resemblance might well be picked up by viewers and go badly for Euan himself. Euan's wife she hadn't seem, so the danger was not so great.

In fact, the temptation did not arise. Jessica found that the casting director had made appointments for five each of the actors and actresses, and it took her the whole day to see them all. None was in the least like Euan, although each matched her requirements in at least some of the characteristics she had stipulated.

Each would have made a good yet individual portrayal of the young Welshman, bringing out different facets of his character; it was Jessica's job to assess just which facets were important for her purpose and which actor would most successfully highlight them.

She did this mostly by talking with the actors, explaining what the film was about, discussing the story and the character of Euan—or Huw, as he was in the story, and taking previous parts played into account. The actors were in general of the class who hadn't yet become household names but kept in fairly steady work, appearing frequently as supporting players in T.V. plays or on the stage. At any moment, for any one of them, might come the break that would bring them stardom, and the eagerness that this knowledge brought them was keeping them all on their toes.

Jessica didn't ask any of them to read her script; she felt that previous track records, plus what she gleaned from her discussions, should be enough. And by the end of the day, she was fairly sure just which ones she wanted to play Huw and Olwen.

'That was wonderful,' she told the casting director as she gathered up her things to leave. 'It was really hard to decide, but I think David Kilbey and Cheryl Martin, if they're going to be free the weeks I'm filming. If not, I'll have to think again, but they're my first choice.'

'Fine,' he said, nodding at her. 'You should have an easier day tomorrow, anyway—only three of each, and one of them's Miles Clayton.'

'Miles Clayton?' Jessica looked at him in surprise. 'Isn't he doing a West End play?'

' 'S right, but he likes to do some T.V. as well and his agent said he was interested in this.' The casting director grinned. 'Shall I tell the others not to come?'

'No—no, that wouldn't be fair.' But as she left the building, Jessica was already feeling excited. Miles Clayton—one of the best-known character actors on the stage today, able to play anything from a scruffy

Yorkshireman to a suave insurance collector. Yes, he'd be ideal for Robert Mercer.

And so he was. As Joe, the casting director, had predicted, the next day was easier and Jessica found herself leaving early, her cast chosen, feeling very satisfied with herself.

Her satisfaction lasted just until she passed the first billboard advertising that day's evening paper. And then her heart seemed to stop and everything to do with the film, her job as director and the rest of the world in its entirety became unimportant.

Revolt in Buwambo, the headlines screamed. *British Archaeological Survey caught in Insurrection*. And on another sheet, fluttering in the wind—*T.V. Crew Missing*.

It was late when Jessica finally arrived back in Shrewsbury. She had gone to London by train, leaving her car at the railway station, and she sighed with relief as she slid into the driving seat and immediately switched on the radio. In five minutes' time there would be a news report and she might find out more about the revolution.

She had learned little from the newspaper. Although it had used the story as its main headline on the newsheets, there was little known about the uprising. The African state was a small one, its name unfamiliar to most people, and there had never been trouble there before. All that the report, which she discovered at last in the Stop Press on the back page, could tell her was that the present government had been overthrown by some unknown agency and that a British T.V. crew, led by producer Matt Fenwood, and an archaeological survey team including anthropologist Chantal Gordon, were in the area. Little more, in fact, than the newsheets had blazed to her horrified eyes.

Jessica had spent the journey in an agony of wild imaginings. Every story she had ever heard about the atrocities committed in revolutions came into her mind; she saw Matt caught in a screaming, hysterical throng, stoned, trampled on, torn to pieces. The vivid pictures had sickened her, but she was unable to stop herself from conjuring them up. What did revolutionaries do to foreigners unlucky or unwise enough to get involved with them? What had the state's relations been with Britain before the insurrection? Presumably good, for the survey team to have been allowed to go there. So did that mean they would now be bad? Did it mean that any Britons would be considered enemies? Who were the insurgents, anyway? And when would there be some news—the newspaper had said that no communications were coming out of Buwambo at all.

The radio news came on as Jessica turned out of the station yard, and she twisted the knob for more volume, waiting breathlessly for the revolution to be mentioned. But first the announcer's calm, measured tones dealt with a riot that had taken place after a football match earlier that evening, and the car strike. Then he turned to the revolution.

'There is still no news of the Britons missing after the rising in Buwambo. The situation seems to have quietened now and there have been no more reports of fighting. It is not yet known who now has command of the country's army.'

Oh, God! So there had been fighting. How could he talk about it so *calmly*? That was Matt out there— Matt, her husband! Matt, who might at this very moment by lying dead, lost to her for ever. . . .

Jessica made up her mind and turned towards the T.V. studios. There was no way she could just go back to the cottage and wait for news. There was only one thing she could do—only one thing she could bear to do. Go to Mercia T.V. and wait in the newsroom until something came through. She had to know—the moment news arrived, she had to be there.

But of course, she couldn't be. There was no knowing

when the news would come—it might be days before
anything more was heard. Or even longer, she thought,
repressing a shudder at the memory of people who had
disappeared in troubled African states and simply never
been heard of again. Was that going to happen to
Matt? Oh no—please God, no, she prayed as she paced
restlessly about among the telex machines and
typewriters until at last she was persuaded to go home
and get some sleep.

'We'll be in touch the minute we hear anything,'
Harry Dalby promised her, looking sympathetically at
her huge shadowed eyes. 'But you can't stay here for
ever—not that you'll need to,' he added hastily, 'there's
bound to be some news soon. But you go and get some
rest, Jess. There's nothing you can do now and you may
need your strength when there is.'

'Yes, all right,' Jessica acknowledged dully. 'Not that
there will be anything I can do. Matt and I are getting a
divorce, you know.'

'No, I didn't know.' He looked at her curiously. 'I
heard that you were getting back together—you're
doing a film for him, aren't you?'

Jessica nodded, but she was too tired and anxious to
argue with him, or to tell him the truth, though she'd
known Harry for years. There would be time for that
later—and anyway, if Matt came back it would be clear
to everyone when he divorced Jessica and married
Chantal. Because that was what was going to happen,
she was convinced. You didn't go through the kind of
experiences he and Chantal must be sharing now and not
come out of it even closer than you were before. And
they were close, there was no doubt about that. Look at
that item in the paper, only a few days ago.

Jessica drove home like an automaton. Her mind was
totally absorbed, coming to grips not only with the
danger Matt must be in at this moment and the
possibility, which had to be faced, that he might never
return—but also with the knowledge that if he did

return, it wouldn't be to Jessica. There had never been much hope for them, she thought sadly, and now it had vanished altogether. Along with the days and nights they had spent in France, it was just a dream. And for the first time she realised that, for four long and lonely years, she had been subconsciously hoping for just that. A miracle—the miracle of their love renewed, refreshed and strengthened.

In spite of everything, she had never stopped loving Matt. Her own pain had made her reject him, hadn't allowed her to admit her love, but it had been there all the same—lying dormant, waiting for the chance to reassert itself. That was why she had never been able to respond to any other man.

It had begun to awaken when Matt had first come back into her life, just a few weeks ago. In spite of all her attempts to deny it, her love had struggled to get to the surface. That phone call the other night might have had her once more at Matt's feet, if she hadn't seen the gossip item immediately afterwards.

But the news of the revolution had swept away all her doubts, all her attempts to keep Matt out of her life. And she could no longer hide from the truth. She loved Matt as much, as deeply and strongly, as ever she had done. And, one way or another, she had lost him. And she would spend the rest of her life knowing it.

The next few days stretched into weeks and still there was no news from Buwambo. Jessica's first sharp anxiety slowly became a gnawing ache that had somehow to be pushed to the back of her mind as everyday life claimed attention. She still switched on the news at every possible opportunity, but after the first week or so, when the new régime in Buwambo had not only settled down but had been recognised by other governments, the missing Britons were scarcely mentioned. All that was possible was being done to trace them, Jessica was assured when she made desperate enquiries through the Foreign Office, and with that she had to be satisfied.

'The only thing I can do is get on with the film,' she told Chris as they had a brief lunch together in a wine bar one day. 'At least it's something I can do for Matt—it's something he wanted me to do. It might be the last——' Her voice shook and she picked up her glass and drank hastily.

'Jessica, don't talk like that! They'll be all right—it's just that things have been so upset and communications are still bad—they'll turn up, I'm sure they will.' Chris put his hand on hers and held it tightly, and Jessica swallowed hard, bit her lip and then met his eyes gratefully.

'Yes, of course. I just get a bit hysterical at times. It's been so long. But I know you're right—it's a case of no news is good news really. Matt will come back.'

'And when he does?' Chris looked down at the table. 'You'll be getting back together?' His tone was casual—almost too casual.

Jessica shook her head. 'Oh, no, there's no chance of that. We've been separated nearly five years now, Chris. We never bothered about divorce before, but now—well, there's Chantal, you see. I imagine she and Matt will want to get married as soon as possible.'

'Chantal?' Chris stared at her, his blue eyes surprised. 'But I thought—well, the way you've been worrying about Matt, it seemed——'

'As if we had some understanding?' Jessica finished for him. 'As if once this trip was over we'd be making a new start? No, Chris, it isn't like that at all. There's no chance of Matt and me trying again. That's definitely all over. Chantal's his lady now, and who can blame him?'

'So—why——?'

'Why have I been getting in such a state? Because I love him, of course.' Jessica paused for a moment, playing with the stem of her wineglass. 'I've been an idiot for four years, Chris. I wouldn't face up to the fact. Now I've had to. And the fact that I've lost Matt doesn't stop me loving him. I don't think it ever will.'

Chris stared at her, then took her hand again. His eyes were grave as he said, 'I didn't realise it was like that, Jessica. I'm sorry.' He hesitated, then said quietly: 'This probably isn't at all the right time to tell you this, but—well, if it's any help to you, you might as well know that I'm around. Whatever happens—I'm here. On your terms; I realise you could never feel for me the way you feel for Matt. Or even the way I feel——'

'Chris, stop! Don't say any more.' He didn't need to, Jessica thought as she gazed at the serious face. She knew exactly what he was telling her, and it was a complication she just couldn't handle right now. 'Just leave it for now, Chris,' she added quietly.

He nodded. 'I did say it wasn't the right time, didn't I? But I think you understand me, Jessica. Sue and I— well, we're all washed up, and——'

'Chris, *please*!' Determinedly, Jessica removed her hand from his and poured him the last of the wine. 'Look, I'd like to get back to the office and finish working on that schedule. We're filming in two days and there are still a lot of loose ends to tie up. Now, what do you think about that local councillor in Montgomery? It seemed to me he'd make a good interview, but when can we fit him in?' Thank God for work, she thought as she and Chris walked back, deep in discussion. If it did nothing else, it filled the time— and it kept Chris from making any more confessions that might embarrass them both.

Despondently, she wondered if Chris could really be in love with her. If he was, if he and Sue really were finished, could they have any future together?

But she couldn't even think about that now—now with Matt missing. Until she knew he was safe, nothing else really mattered.

The filming began, and Jessica had to admit that she was pleased by the smoothness of it all. Weeks of meticulous planning were now paying off as the crew travelled about, taking atmospheric shots of the Welsh countryside and filming the various interviews that had been arranged. By this time, Jessica had had several more talks with Euan Parry, and had done a sound interview, though she was hoping also to use him on film in some way as well. She found herself now firmly on his side, bitterly resentful of the system which had allowed such situations to arise, and the direction of the film showed this attitude, especially in her interviews.

Chris was clearly disturbed by this and tried to redress the balance by using his own opportunities to phrase quesions in a way that would present an alternative point of view. Jessica's interviewing technique helped him there; neither of them was actually to appear on film as an interviewer, neither would their questions be heard, the viewer seeing only the interviewee apparently musing alone. When the interview was actually recorded, both Jessica and Chris were asking questions, though Chris's were intended as a back-up in case Jessica forgot an important point.

Once filming had started, it took precedence over everything else, starting early in the morning and finishing usually some time during the evening. The entire crew travelled in a fleet of cars, staying at the same hotels and generally eating together in the evenings before falling exhausted into bed. The world outside seemed to have little relevance; their world had become this tight little circle intent only on doing a good job, and nothing else was allowed to impinge upon it.

Nevertheless, Jessica couldn't forget Matt. Each night, as soon as she could, she escaped to her room and switched on the radio for news. But there never was any; only the eternal round of strikes and accidents and political chicanery, and none of these held the slightest interest for Jessica.

Was there never going to be news of Matt? she wondered despairingly. Was he really going to become nothing more than a statistic—another in the number of people who had vanished without trace somewhere or other in the world, never to be heard of again?

Perhaps it would be better to stop listening. Accept that he had dropped out of her life for ever, and forget this aching, desperate hope that was tearing her apart, cutting off her appetite and intruding on her sleep. Accept that she had seen him for the last time in his office with Chantal; heard his voice for the last time over the long-distance telephone; kissed him for the last time. . . .'

Abruptly, Jessica wrenched her mind away from the thoughts that circled so endlessly around it, and tried to concentrate on her work. Tomorrow was to be the first of the dramatised sequences shot at the Hartes' cottage overlooking the Mawdacch estuary. She had already spent some time in rehearsing with the actors and felt happy that they were all in tune and understood the characters they were playing. This was the most exciting part of the film, and she had looked forward to it from the beginning.

The scenes in the Hartes' cottage involved only the older couple, except for one scene when Huw came to look at it just before setting fire to it; he was seen from inside, peering through the windows, his eyes widening as he took in the improvements that had been made, the now luxurious interior of what had been a very simple cottage. As he looked, his expression slowly changed from a wistful yearning to a savage jealousy. This was the tiny home where he had hoped to start his married life, his savings just enough to meet the kind of price that would have been realistic. Instead, it had been sold for a much higher price to a rich businessman, to be used for holidays and weekends. There would be no children brought up here, as Huw had hoped to bring up his own family. And now, because of the fashion for holiday cottages or 'second homes', his own life had been ruined. He had been unable to find even a first home and had been driven to the city to find work. There, stultified by the crowded streets and the shabby flat, his young wife had grown more and more unhappy until she had at last lost the baby they had both longed for, and finally returned home to her parents.

All this had to show in Huw's face as he looked in through the windows at the kind of luxury he could never afford. With no dialogue, it was a measure of the actor's skill that he was able to do this; and with Euan's own words as voice-over, the whole scene would be highly effective.

The scene would be very short when finally shown, but it nevertheless took a considerable time to film. As Huw was to be seen looking through several windows, camera and lights had to be set up in each room, and this was a process that took time and care. Added to which, some of the takes were spoilt by things over which they had no control; sound of a train chugging across the bridge below, an aeroplane suddenly deafening them all as it zoomed overhead, the sudden frenzied barking of two dogs having a fight close to the garden wall. These were all the kind of interruptions that were normal on such occasions and everyone took them in good part, but they made the day a long one and Jessica was very tired when she finally collapsed into her bed at the local hotel.

Still, she was pleased with the way the day had gone. David Kilbey, the actor playing Huw, had made a good start and she was sure that his thin, haunted face was going to make a considerable impression on the viewers. And Miles Clayton, playing the businessman, would be the perfect foil; he could look sleekly prosperous, even smug, while still coming over convincingly as the man who cared for nothing as much as he cared for his crippled wife. The scenes she intended shooting tomorrow, with Miles and Margaret Warran, who played his wife Jane, should go well. Both were experienced and accomplished actors and they had worked together before.

There was to be no shooting at the weekend, when the cottage scenes were over; Jessica had considered carrying on through Saturday but decided that the crew would benefit from a rest. She was also uncomfortably aware that the budget was now getting very tight, several unexpected expenses having arisen, and wanted to avoid incurring too much in the way of overtime. Hilary, who as production assistant was in charge of the day-to-day expenses, had also expressed some concern.

'This fire scene is proving terribly expensive,' she had told Jessica earlier that day. 'The local authorities certainly mean to make it pay its way—even though we're saving them trouble in demolishing the place! I suppose you can't blame them, they don't get T.V. companies subsidising the rates every day of the week, but it's running us awfully tight.'

'Well, we'll just have to watch it in the other scenes,' said Jessica. 'No use spoiling the ship for a ha'porth of tar. I want to make a good job of this film, Hilary.' Not just want to—have to, she added silently. And if she had wanted to do that before, as a means of impressing Matt. she needed to even more now that she had come in her heart to believe it would be the last thing she could do for him.

Suppressing the thought, she pulled the filming schedule towards her. 'Let's just go over what we're doing tomorrow,' she said. 'The scene with the Mercers first viewing the cottage—we don't shoot that here, it has to be the other one. Interiors—we can't use the living-room for that, but we can use that room they keep their boxes and tings in—clear it out and put a few old pieces of furniture in and it'll look quite tatty. Have we got the old furniture?'

'Yes, that's all arranged. And the little scullery could be used too. The Hartes haven't done much to that as it's so small and bare anyway.'

'Mm. It's been painted, though. Trouble is, T.V. always makes things look so good—I remember once doing a shot of what was supposed to be a really scruffy bed-sitting room, in a studio. The director thought the original design looked too smart on film, so we tried to make it look worse—and whatever we did to it, it looked better! I wouldn't have minded living there myself in the end. We had to admit that the designer was right in the first place and go back to his original set.'

'Yes, I've known that happen too,' Hilary agreed, smiling. 'It's an advantage in permanent sets—like news studios, which do get quite scruffy but always look fine on screen. But it can be a problem otherwise.'

'Well, we'll have to see how the cottage looks tomorrow. It doesn't have to look too bad, of course—just a bit shabby.' Jessica got up and stretched. 'I think that's it for now. You know, I've a good mind to have dinner in my room tonight—just an omelette or something. I'm shattered!'

But even so, tired as she was, she found it difficult to sleep. She lay in bed, half awake, her mind haunted by restless images she couldn't quite capture yet couldn't push away. And when she did fall into an uneasy slumber her dreams reflected her anxiety and she seemed to spend the entire night trying desperately to pack endless suitcases to go on a journey she knew she would never make.

Jessica was thankful, as she unlocked the door of her cottage, that she had decided against any filming at the weekend. The past three days, following the rehearsals and the interviews she had done the previous week, had taken their toll and she felt that once back in her own bed she would sleep until Monday morning. Directing was certainly hard work; every moment had to be planned in advance, even though her plans were quite likely to be foiled by unforeseen snags, so that she had to be prepared at any moment to change her mind and take advantage of the new situation. *If they hand you a lemon, use it to make lemonade,* she quoted ruefully to herself. Well, there was certainly a lot of lemonade in a director's life. And nobody else to help make it; helpful though people like Chris, Hilary, the cameramen and the floor manager might be, the ultimate decision at all times must be hers. She had to carry responsibility.

She knew now why Matt had been less than enthusiastic about her ambition to direct. He'd known just what hard work it was, how exacting and, if things went wrong, how thankless. He'd known just how easy it was to make the wrong decision, knew how easily she could be hurt. Perhaps he had been, as she had accused him, over-protective—but he wouldn't have been if he hadn't loved her, would he? Being over-protective, particularly in such a stressful world as T.V., wasn't a marital crime, after all. Not like unfaithfulness.

As she moved slowly about the kitchen, making herself a light meal, Jessica tried to forget Matt's infidelity, but the memory was all too insistent. Why had he turned to other women, when he had apparently loved her enough to want to protect her from getting hurt? Was he simply the kind of man who couldn't help it, who needed women and sex as he needed three meals a day and couldn't be expected to go without either just because his wife wasn't around to provide them? A womaniser, indiscriminate and incorrigible? Jessica thought about it, then shook her head. She would never have believed that Matt was like that. He was too strong, too disciplined. And he was a man of principle; a man of integrity. Or so she had always believed.

That was what had hurt her so much, of course. She had trusted him implicitly, believing that once he had married her he would never look at another woman, believing that no mere physical separation would drive a wedge between them. Yet at the first test, when he had gone to Finland with the pretty new production assistant, Fiona, the rumours had started. And they'd continued, growing and forcing themselves on her attention no matter how she tried to ignore them, until the climax of his affair—there was no other word for it—with the beautiful actress Sylvia Steele in New York.

Bitterly hurt and jealous, Jessica had been unable to bear any more. She had fled, giving him no chance to make excuses, and shut him out of her heart. Or tried to. For over four years, she had thought she had succeeded; it was only now, with Matt irrevocably lost to her, that she admitted he had kept possession of her heart all that time.

So why had he turned to those others? Could it in some way have been her fault? For the first time in four years, Jessica began tentatively to examine her own behaviour. She had never done so before; her bitter anger had all been directed towards Matt. Now, as she carried her plate through to the living-room and set a match to the fire already laid in the stone fireplace, she wondered just what it was about her that had turned away Matt's love.

Perhaps she had been too ambitious. But why not? she argued defensively—this was the twentieth century, not the days of Jane Austen. Women did all kinds of things and men were, at last, beginning to accept that— weren't they? Matt had certainly seemed to expect her to be his wife first and foremost, though he'd been happy enough to allow her to continue working as a P.A.—so long as she worked for him.

No, there was no reason why marriage should have stopped Jessica's career in its tracks, any more than Matt's. But perhaps she could have asserted herself more subtly, been less arrogant about it. The gentle touch, she thought wryly as she sipped her coffee. She'd never considered it necessary—had just assumed that Matt would recognise her rights, and then been angry when he hadn't.

So there was fault on both sides, perhaps. Matt had grown tired of living with a shrew and turned to more compliant women. But there was little use in recognising this now—when she knew she would never have the chance to put things right. And she sat staring desolately into the fire, watching the leaping flames without really seeing them at all, as she thought sadly and hopelessly of what might have been.

The flames licked higher, yellow and bright; then died to a glowing red. Its soft light touched Jessica's face and reached into the shadowy corners of the room. A soft, companionable hissing came from the mixture of coal and wood, and every now and then there was a crackle as it shifted in the grate, and a tiny spurt of flame. But Jessica was aware of none of this. Worn out by the week's filming and by her gnawing anxiety about Matt, she had slipped to the hearthrug and, her cheek resting on the cushions of the chair she leaned against, was fast asleep.

She woke suddenly, her heart leaping in alarm as she wondered dazedly just where she was. Her cheek was numb, her arms stiff from their camped position, and there were pins and needles in her legs. The fire had died right down, just a dull glow coming from its ashes, and the room was chilly. Jessica sat up awkwardly, rubbing her legs, and pushing back the tawny hair that had fallen around her face. And then she stiffened in fear.

Someone was in the room with her. Someone had come into the cottage while she slept and now stood just inside the door, watching her. It was too dark to see his face and his body loomed like a giant's in the shadowed room, but he was moving closer and she could only stare up at him in paralysed terror. There was nothing she could do—nothing. And although he knew that his size indicated a strength that could overpower her with ease, her fingers reached blindly for the poker. At least she had to try!

'Leave it alone,' he said softly. 'Don't do anything you'd regret, Jessica. Aren't you pleased to see me again?'

The soft velvety tones struck at her like a blow. She knew them—she had last heard them over a telephone call, coming to her from thousands of miles away. But it couldn't be—it wasn't possible—it was a trick, a hoax, it had to be. And then he touched her; trailed his fingertips through her cloud of hair, found her neck, turned her face up to his; and she knew that it must be true.

'*Matt!*' she whispered on a thread of sound, and then the shadows merged about her into a solid darkness and she felt her body sag into oblivion.

CHAPTER SEVEN

'FEELING better?'

Jessica opened her eyes and stared at the face that looked down at her. The dark, waving hair ... the grey eyes, soft as summer clouds ... the high, intelligent forehead ... the mouth that was tight with anxiety now but broke into its quirky grin even as she looked. ... So it hadn't been a dream.

'Matt?' she breathed wonderingly, and he nodded. 'Oh, *Matt*!'

Without another thought, she reached up and flung her arms round his neck, drawing him down to her, pulling him close. His chin was rough with stubble and she rubbed her face against it, delighting in the friction, then found his lips and met them wholeheartedly, without reserve. All the loneliness, the longing and despair of the past weeks went into her kiss then, and through the joyful surging of her blood that sounded like a thundering ocean in her ears, she heard Matt utter a sudden groan, a groan that seemed torn from his heart as a hurricane tears a great tree from its roots. She felt his arms reach for her, jerking her even closer as his weight came down on her body and she thrilled again to the sensation of his hard, masculine body pressed against hers, moving sensuously as they moulded to each other, rediscovering forgotten delights, each remembering little movements and caresses that had once pleased the other. The world outside receded and disappeared; the only reality was here in this room, the only secret the one shared by them both.

Matt shifted his weight away from Jessica and looked down at her. His eyes were shadowed, the grey of a falcon's wing, and her heart leapt at the expression in them. Slowly, he brushed back her mass of coppery hair, letting it trail through his fingers strand by silken strand until it was spread out around her head, glowing in the firelight. Then, his hand cupping her face, he bent and kissed her again; a series of tiny kisses, planted like spots of fire over her cheeks, eyelids, forehead, nose and chin, before moving down to the hollow of her throat where her pulse beat as strongly as a bird's wings. His lips explored her neck, his teeth nipped at the lobes of her ears, and his hands moved down over her body, cupping each breast, moulding them in his curving palms, his fingertips finding the shape of the nipples under the fine wool of her sweater, testing their hardness with sensuality that had Jessica whimpering with pleasure, thrusting herself against him and pulling his face up to hers so that she could kiss his mouth and express her own longing and desire.

Matt grunted deep in his throat and slid his hand under her sweater, pulling it over her head and removing her lacy bra almost in the same movement. For a long moment his eyes rested on Jessica's swelling breasts, then as she shivered involuntarily he turned away from her and dragged several small logs from the basket by the hearth. They caught as soon as he threw them on the fire, and he turned back to her, his eyes once again on her body as the flames threw their flickering warmth on to her skin.

'God, you're lovely, Jessica,' he muttered, trailing his fingers across her naked rosiness. 'Even lovelier than I remembered—and God knows I've remembered often enough. . . .' His fingers reached the waistband of her jeans and undid the fastenings, then slid the denim down over her hips and thighs. 'You've been losing weight,' he said with sudden sharpness. 'Why's that?'

Worrying about you, Jessica wanted to answer, but she couldn't speak. The thundering excitement of being here with Matt, letting him undress her, seemed to be almost choking her, so that her breath came quick and shallow and her senses reeled and for a few moments she wondered if she might be going to faint again. And then Matt had finished his delicious task and was gazing down at her, his eyes taking in every intimate detail of her body, and if he didn't come back to her soon and hold her and kiss her again she didn't know how she was going to bear it.

But his own undressing was swift. Almost before she was ready, he was beside her again, stretched out on the rug, his heart beating strongly against hers, the flames rippling now on his muscular leanness, his body a curious mixture of hardness and pliability, Jessica wound her arms around him, exulting in the feel of their skins touching, and for a while they simply rocked together in the warmth, aware of every inch of contact, exploring each other's body with mind as much as physical sense, content to be close yet learning to be even closer.

But this could not be enough for long. Soon their hands had begun to move again, caressingly, touching at first with gentle wonder, then with increasing passion as their lips met again, moving with a fierce longing that would not be denied. Matt gathered her against him, handling her body as if she were a doll, curving her to his own contours, then stretched her arms above her head, one hand holding her by the wrists, the other sliding its sensuous way down from palm to thigh; and then, slipping it under her body, he arched her towards him. A great wave of desire swept over Jessica and she twined her legs around his body and met him in his last fierce assault, a cry of triumphant ecstasy bursting from their throats in a simultaneous climax of joy as they moved together in a pulsing rhythm in which their bodies seemed to have taken full control.

Neither of them could have said how long it lasted. Jessica was only aware of a searing happiness that came to her in a series of explosions, each one more shattering than the last, until the final glorious sunburst that left her limp and exhausted in Matt's arms, arms and legs still entwined but with no more energy left in them; lips resting against his neck, ears filled with the roaring of her pulses, heart drumming in her breast like a wild animal fighting its way from a cage.

The flames had died down and the logs almost burned away before either of them moved again; and then, at last, Matt stirred and said softly: 'That was some welcome home!'

'Oh, Matt,' Jessica whispered, settling deeper in his arms, 'I thought you were dead. I thought I'd lost you!'

She felt him move and opened her eyes to see him raised on one elbow, gazing down at her.

'And would that have been so bad?'

'Yes,' she breathed. 'I didn't know how I was going to bear it.' She paused, the memory of the past weeks washing over her. 'I knew I'd lost you anyway—but I couldn't bear it if you were dead—if there was no hope at all.'

'Lost me?' Matt repeated. 'How do you mean, lost me?'

'Well——' Jessica licked her lips, reluctant to bring even Chantal's name into this room that was still warm with their lovemaking, 'I thought—you and Chantal——'

An expression she couldn't read crossed Matt's face, and she stopped, half afraid, as he bent closer. But as he laid his lips on hers, she heard him mutter: 'We won't talk about Chantal, Jessica. This night is for us. Come closer, darling ... kiss me again. ...' And as her lips parted, the excitement surged through her body again and with an incredulous delight she realised that their loving wasn't over, it was beginning again; and if, this second time, it was less fierce, less tumultuous than it had been before, it was certainly no less consuming. Instead, it was gentle, familiar, comfortable. And when it was over, there was no exhaustion; just a warm sleepiness and the secure contentment of lying closely entwined, two boneless bodies that fitted together as if made for each other, curling together like puppies on the rug in front of the slowly dying fire.

Jessica woke to find a pale spring sunshine filling the room with light. She was no longer curled into the warmth of Matt's body, but was covered by a feathery duvet which fitted snugly round her bare skin. She raised her head, still half asleep and dazed by the night's loving, and saw Matt, dressed in dark slacks and a polo-necked sweater, just putting a match to a freshly-laid fire.

She put out a hand and touched him and he turned and smiled at her.

'Hullo. What's that for?'

'Just making sure you're real.' Jessica shifted and found that her body, even in a duvet, was stiff. 'Whew, this floor's hard!'

'Even a sheepskin rug doesn't quite match up to a bed,' Matt agreed. 'For sleeping on, that is. It makes a very good substitute in other ways. . . .' He bent and kissed her lightly on the lips. 'How about breakfast in bed?'

'No, thanks.' Jessica sat up, still holding the duvet around her, feeling suddenly shy. 'I think I've been on this rug long enough.'

'I didn't say anything about staying here,' he murmured, drawing his fingers slowly and sensuously down her throat. 'I said, in bed.' His lips parted hers before she could answer and she rested against him, helpless in his arms, her heart fluttering into her throat as his tongue teased hers.

'Matt. . . .' she murmured weakly, and he laughed softly.

'The electric blanket's switched on,' he murmured persuasively. 'And the coffee's ready in the pot. We don't need any more than that, do we? If I remember rightly, you always did prefer love and kisses to bacon and eggs, hm?' His mouth found hers again. 'It's a diet any doctor would recommend,' he whispered, and Jessica closed her eyes.

'Matt ... don't you think we should talk?' she pleaded between kisses, but he shook his head vigorously.

'We can talk any time. Just now, all I want is ... this.' Jessica gasped as his fingers probed delicately beneath the duvet. 'And it's what you want, too, isn't it?' he added with the sureness of experience as she shuddered with desire and let her fingers clutch convulsively at his shoulders. Gently, he disengaged himself and rose lithely to his feet. 'Come on, Jessica. It's Saturday—remember? The day when we always had a lie-in. It was a good habit—let's get back into it.' And he lifted her easily in his arms and carried her from the room and up the narrow stairs, laying her gently in the warm, wide bed.

It was almost noon when she woke again. The sunshine had moved round the cottage, but she could see that it was still a bright day outside, the branches of the trees with their fresh greening of young leaves dancing in the breeze. Matt had opened a window before joining her in the bed, and she could hear the singing of birds as they went about the business of building their nests—the robin she had told Matt about over the phone, the tits and a thrush. She lay still, letting the quiet pleasure of an English spring day warm her heart, and then she turned her head on the pillow to look at Matt.

He was still asleep, lying on his side facing her, one arm flung across her body, dark hair hiding his face. Gently, Jessica drew back the duvet and looked at his body, her eyes moving slowly over the broad shoulders, the well-muscled back tapering to a narrow waist and hips. His skin was bronzed a rich brown from the African sun, but she was curiously relieved to note the white mark of his shorts, standing out against the deep tan of his powerful thighs. Just what had happened out there in Africa? she wondered. Not with Chantal—Matt had made it clear he didn't want to talk about the blonde anthropologist—but during the uprising. What dangers had he faced, what perils had he escaped? And the rest of the crew, too—were they all safe? Even Chantal, she had to admit, she would not have wished any harm, and she hoped with all the generosity that she could now afford to offer the other woman that they had all reached home safely.

Matt stirred and turned on his back, his hand trailing over Jessica's naked body as he did so. The sensation made her shiver, and Matt felt it too; he frowned slightly, then opened his eyes and looked at the ceiling. Then he turned his head and saw Jessica looking down at him. They stared at each other without moving.

'Yes, it is true,' Matt said at last. 'I know now how you felt—I want to touch you, make sure you're really there and it's not just another dream.'

Another dream? Jessica thought, but aloud she said, 'Go ahead—I've no objection.'

'I wouldn't expect you to have any, you little witch,' he said, laughing at her dancing eyes. 'But I think it's safer to keep my distance. You're wearing me out, you know that?' He studied her face for a moment, then muttered roughly: 'Oh, what the hell! Let's get worn out together!' and dragged her down on top of him.

Laughing, Jessica let him kiss her for a few minutes, then wriggled out of his arms. 'I don't think I want you to wear out,' she declared, escaping from the duvet and standing before him. 'And I want some more coffee. And perhaps even something to eat!'

'Don't stand there like that, then,' he growled, 'or I'll be tempted to eat you! Make yourself decent, woman. And get to your rightful place!'

'And that is?' Jessica hastily wrapped a white bathrobe round her and evaded his reaching hands.

'The kitchen, of course. Don't you know the way to a man's heart is through his stomach?'

'Funny,' she murmured, slipping through the door, 'I thought I'd found another route. . . . All right, all right, I'm going! Omelette do you? Or would you rather I spent a couple of happy hours knocking up something more exotic?'

'You're quite exotic enough for me to cope with,' he retorted, appearing behind her as she made for the bathroom. 'The human male can only take so much, you know . . . and this particular human male isn't really going to notice what he's eating anyway,' he added softly, wrapping his arms around her and giving her a kiss that had her shaking with tenderness. 'Jess, it's good to be back with you.'

'It's good to have you back,' she answered unsteadily. 'I—I didn't know how much I'd missed you.'

'No, I know.' His grey eyes held hers, then he turned her round and pushed her gently through the bathroom door. 'Go along, now. We'll talk later—but for now, just let's enjoy it, right?' And as she nodded dumbly, he closed the door quietly, leaving her alone with her chaotic thoughts.

They spent the day in a dream of loving rediscovery. By tacit consent, they didn't mention Chantal again, but talked instead of the happy times they had had in the past, moving on as their confidence in each other grew to the years they had spent apart. Matt described some of the TV programmes and films he had produced, including the famous *Nature Search* which Jessica found fascinating. It had taken him all over the world and although there had been a great deal of tedium and discomfort to endure, there had also been moments of pure magic, and it was these moments which had been translated to the screen and held the nation in thrall. 'Especially in South America,' he recalled. 'You see so many of these nature films done in Africa, and admittedly it's a paradise for the naturalist—but there are places in South America that have hardly been touched, animals and birds and plants that haven't even been named yet. And there's such a range of geography, too—from the icebergs of the Horn to the tropical Amazon jungle. Now that's a place I certainly want to go back to some day.'

'It sounds wonderful,' Jessica murmured, and she felt him smile in her hair.

'Then maybe we'll go together. Though I won't ask you to come as my P.A. this time—but perhaps as director, hm?'

When it grew dark they made up the fire again and Matt went outside for more logs. The spring weather, though bright, had turned cold and the evening air was almost frosty. Hope the weather stays like this, Jessica thought vaguely. It would be ideal for the week's filming. But all that seemed a long way away, somehow. There was still another whole day and two blissful nights to go before she need think about work, and she was determined to make the most of every single minute.

It wasn't until much later, as they sat together gazing into the fire, that she asked Matt how he had escaped from Buwambo.

'I was frantic,' she told him, her arms tightening round his body. 'There just wasn't any news at all—I didn't think I'd ever see you again, and there was just nothing I could do about it.'

'It wasn't too good,' Matt admitted. 'Though we were never in any real danger—we didn't even know there'd been an insurrection until it was all over! We were right out in the bush, you see, and apparently nobody gave us a thought. But when we did hear about it we had quite a problem on our hands. Because our excavations had been a sore point with the new régime and we didn't expect much of a welcome if we went strolling back into the city once they were in power. So we had to find another way out.'

He spoke casually, but Jessica, watching his face, knew that the situation could have been grim. 'What did you do?' she asked tensely.

'Walked.' His laconic voice gave no hint of the privations they must have endured. Jessica pictured it—the long trek to the border, perhaps hundreds of miles away, with the sun beating mercilessly down on them. ... 'That sounds terrible!' she exclaimed. 'How far was it? And what about food and water?'

'It was far enough,' he admitted. 'And we had to watch out for troops—we guessed they wouldn't have much sympathy with us. We didn't do too badly, though. Don't forget, we'd been working on an excavation, we had wheelbarrows and things. There wasn't any use in trying to use a vehicle, for one thing there wasn't enough fuel to carry us all out and for another we didn't want to attract attention. But a wheelbarrow doesn't make much noise or dust. We packed them up with food and water, and just set off, leaving everything we didn't need. It was pretty gruelling, but we survived—it wasn't too far to the border and once across it we were on friendly territory. The worst part was leaving the dig, just when it was getting interesting. I hope we can go back some time—there's something big there and I want to be filming it when it's finally unearthed.'

'And I suppose all the gear's lost, too,' said Jessica. 'The filming gear as well as the archaeological stuff.'

'Oh no,' said Matt with a grin. 'We didn't leave that. We made quite a nice little film of the whole thing. It's being shown soon.' He glanced at Jessica, a puzzled frown creasing his high forehead. 'Jess, when you saw me you passed clean out. Didn't you think I'd come to you the first moment I could?'

'I don't understand,' Jessica said. 'I told you, I'd made up my mind you were dead—that I was never going to see you again. When I saw you there, I thought for a minute you were a ghost. Of course I fainted!'

'Then you didn't know I was safe?' She shook her head. 'Had you given up listening to the news?'

'You mean they *reported* it?' Jessica stared at him, thinking of all the times she'd hurried frantically to a radio or T.V. to see if there had been any news of the missing Britons. And then, despairing, she had given up. Those past three days, she hadn't turned the radio on at all. 'I could have known,' she said slowly. 'I could have known you were safe. That much worry at least I could have spared myself.'

'And been prepared,' he said quietly. 'And by the time I arrived all those defences would have been up in place again and I would never have seen that wonderful, real and honest reaction. Jess, I'm glad you didn't know! Aren't you?'

And Jessica, knowing that what he said was true, could only murmur yes as once again his lips sought hers and they slipped easily, comfortably and yet as excitedly as new lovers into the rhythm of their passion.

It was late on Sunday afternoon when Matt finally left, and then it was only because he had an appointment at the studios early next morning and needed to collect some papers from his flat in London before then.

'I'll spend the night there and then drive back,' he said as he and Jessica stood at the cottage door saying goodbye. 'And after that, we'll get ourselves sorted out. What are you doing this week, Jessica?'

'Filming,' she said wryly, thinking how odd it was that she hadn't even mentioned her work to Matt. But there had been too much else to talk about; and too much to do. . . . 'It's the second week. I hope to get it finished by the weekend.'

'My God, of course! And I've never even asked you how it was going.' Matt pulled a comically apologetic face. 'But we haven't even had that talk we promised ourselves, have we? The time's gone so fast. . . .'

'There's plenty more of it,' Jessica assured him

steadily. 'All we need. We'll talk next weekend, Matt, when this is finished. And meantime—will I be seeing you again?'

Matt grinned down at her and bent his head for a kiss. 'You'd better believe it!' he murmured huskily. 'In fact, I may change my mind about spending the night in London. I could just come straight back . . . I needn't get up so early in the morning then, need I! What do you think?'

'I think it would be very nice,' she whispered demurely. 'But don't take any chances, Matt. Not for just one night.'

'Honey,' he said, 'I've walked half across Africa for a night with you. What possible dangers can an English country road hold? I'll be back!' And he gave her another quick, hard kiss and then strode out to his Mercedes, parked close against the hedge. He gave Jessica a wave as he moved smoothly off down the lane, and she stood by the door watching as he went up the valley and along the road, visible across the fields for several minutes before he finally disappeared.

With a little sigh, she went back into the cottage. It felt empty and unnaturally quiet, and she roamed from room to room, reliving every moment since she had first looked up and seen Matt standing in the shadows on Friday evening.

It seemed impossible that she could have been in such depths of despair only two days ago. Impossible that she could have believed Matt lost to her . . . impossible to believe that they could have wasted four long years, when they were capable of giving and receiving from each other such happiness.

Jessica threw another log on the fire and curled up on the soft, shabby sofa in front of it. Some time, she supposed she'd have to get herself a meal, but meanwhile. . . .

She was roused by a violent knocking on the door. Raising her head, she realised that it was almost dark;

she must have fallen asleep. With a sudden jerk of excitement, she glanced at her watch—but it surely couldn't be Matt already. The journey to and from London would take him longer than this, even in that sleek Mercedes. Then who——?

'*Chris!*' she gasped, opening the front door.

Chris peered at her. There was something odd about him, she thought in alarm. His eyes looked strange— unfocussed, bleary. And his face seemed to have slipped in some odd way, as if he weren't in full control. As she stared at him, he leaned forward and lurched slightly, and then she realised what was the matter.

'Chris! You're *drunk!*'

'If you say so,' he agreed with a foolish grin, and Jessica sighed with exasperation.

'You'd better come inside. Look, take my arm—lean on me, that's it. Through here—mind that little table— don't trip over the rug—now, sit down on the sofa, that's right. I'll get you some black coffee.' But as she looked at him, she doubted whether even a gallon of black coffee was going to make much difference in the state he was in. 'Chris, what on earth have you been doing? How did you get in such a condition on a Sunday afternoon?'

'Drank too much,' Chris said succinctly, and Jessica mentally told herself *ask a silly question.* 'Been to see Sue 'n' Jasper.' His mild blue eyes were bewildered as he looked up at Jessica. 'She—she doesn't want me any more, Jess. She doesn't *need* me. She—she's got herself a boy-friend. Another bloke. She don' want to see me any more.' And to Jessica's horror, he put both hands to his face and burst into tears.

'*Chris!*' she gasped, appalled. 'Oh, Chris, don't! Please! Look, maybe it's not as bad as you think— maybe she's just doing it to defy you, to show you she means business—she still wants you back, I'm sure. Don't give up now—oh, don't cry like that, Chris, I can't bear it——'

'I can't bear it either,' he choked. 'It's true, Jess, it's all true—she wants a divorce. I don't want to lose her, Jess—I'd do anything she wants, give up my job, anything—but it's too late now. She told me that. It's too late!'

Jessica stared helplessly at him. Pity overwhelmed her, all the more because of her own newfound happiness. Oh, why couldn't the world be more fair? she asked despairingly. Did someone have to go down so that someone else could go up, like some giant and eternal seesaw? Couldn't everyone be happy at the same time, or would that throw some universal gear out of action? She leaned forward and drew Chris close, her arms round his shoulders, and he sobbed like a child against her breast.

'Look, you'd better have some coffee,' she suggested again. 'You're in no condition to think straight, let alone anything else. I'll go and make it, and then we'll talk.'

But as she'd guessed, Chris was little better after the coffee and Jessica had to admit to herself that he probably wouldn't improve much before morning. And then he would have one hell of a hangover. She watched him as he slumped against the back of the sofa. He really had been hit hard; she'd never known him drink too much before.

Clearly, in spite of what he had said about his feelings for herself, he had really been in love with Sue all the time—just as she had been with Matt. When the crunch came, you certainly knew the truth, she thought ruefully, and wondered if there could be any hope for Chris and Sue, or whether she had really finished with him. Well, that was something only time could tell. It certainly couldn't be sorted out tonight.

Tonight! She looked again at Chris, sitting with his eyes closed now and a look of misery on his pleasant features. What was she going to do with him tonight? There was no possibility of his going back to his hotel in this condition—or anywhere else, for that matter. Behind the wheel of a car, he would be lethal—it must have been only by good luck that he'd reached her cottage safely. There was no way she could send him out again.

So he would have to spend the night here. Doubtfully, Jessica assessed him. He would have to have the bed, she decided reluctantly. He was too tall to sleep comfortably on the sofa, and he was going to feel rotten enough in the morning anyway. Once on the bed he would at least be comfortable, with plenty of room to spread out, and she could settle down here by the fire. There didn't seem to be anything else she could do.

Well, the sooner she got him upstairs the better—he was showing distinct signs of falling asleep, in spite of the black coffee, and once he was off he would probably be nearly comatose and impossible to wake. Sighing, she reached across and shook him by the shoulder, aware that she wasn't a moment too soon—even now he was reluctant to wake and she had to shake him quite violently before he reacted.

'Huh? Whassat? Oh, leave me alone—don't keep bullying me,' he said plaintively, but Jessica gave him another determined shake and dragged him to his feet, where he slumped against her, arms hanging at his sides.

'Oh, *Chris*, for goodness' sake!' Exasperated, Jessica grabbed his hands and looped them round her neck. 'Look, you've got to get upstairs on my bed—co-operate a bit, *please!*' She held him firmly round the waist, her other hand keeping him from sagging forward. 'Come on—one foot forward—now the other, that's right. Now—keep doing it. Careful through the door—and now we're going upstairs. Wake *up*, Chris, just for a few minutes. Mind—you'll have us both over! Look, *that's* it—and again—nearly there—whew!'

Panting with exertion, she guided Chris's stumbling footsteps through the bedroom door and virtually dropped him on the bed. For a few minutes she leaned against the wall, getting back her breath and looking at his prone body, before bending to remove his shoes and swing his feet up on the bed. Then she went to the cupboard to fetch the spare duvet; there was no way she was going to get Chris under the one already on the bed.

By now, he appeared to be fast asleep and impervious to all that she did. But as she spread the duvet over him, he suddenly reached out and grabbed her wrist. Startled, Jessica looked at him and saw that his eyes were open and fixed on her unblinkingly.

'Don't go away,' he said pleadingly. 'Stay here with me.'

'Chris, don't be silly, I can't do that.'

'Why not?' The words were slurred but quite clear, and Jessica sought desperately for words that would persuade him to release that unexpected strong grip on her wrist.

'Chris, you'll be better on your own. Just go to sleep, get some rest. That's what you need now——'

'*You're* what I need now.' The words shocked her into silence. 'Why d'you think I came? You're all I've got left, Jessica—you understand me, you know what it's like. Stay with me, Jessica, please—it's the least you can do, and I don't want to be on my own.'

Oh lord, how do I get out of this? Jessica wondered frantically. She looked at Chris and saw that his eyes were closed, but the grip on her wrist was just as firm and when she tried to pull away it tightened inexorably. She bit her lip and considered. Obviously Chris was going to fall asleep soon, and then his fingers must relax and she would be able to slip away. Wouldn't it be better to give in and stay with him for a while? He was clearly deeply unhappy and needed support—her support. Tomorrow, he would have to know that he couldn't expect anything more, but was there any need to tell him that now—even if he could take it in? Out of her own happiness, couldn't she spare Chris just a few small crumbs?

'All right,' she said gently, 'I'll stay.' And she sat down on the bed beside him.

'No—not like that,' he muttered, jerking at her wrist. 'Lie down—not sit there like a hospital visitor. Lie down with me, Jessica—please.'

Sighing, but seeing no choice, Jessica lay down on top of the duvet. But that wasn't good enough either, and eventually she gave in to his pleas and slid under the duvet with him, slipping her arm under his shoulders and drawing him close. Chris gave a sigh of relief, turned his face into her shoulder and fell fast asleep.

Jessica, exhausted by the stresses of the week, the emotions of the weekend and the pure physical strain of getting Chris up the stairs, waited for his fingers to loosen round her wrist so that she could slip quietly away. But before they did so, she too was asleep; and she didn't wake until the blaze of headlights from a large Mercedes saloon swept across the room. And before she had gathered her dazed wits and realised what they meant, the sound of the front door opening and closing, followed by the steady thud of footsteps on the stairs, told her that the worst had happened. Matt had been as good as his word and driven straight back from London. And she could only hope that he would believe the truth of her story.

Matt was at the bedroom door before Jessica could move. Still under the duvet, with Chris cuddled against her side like a child, she could only blink helplessly up at him as he snapped the light on and stared down at her, his face a study of incredulous disbelief. As his expression changed, hardening to anger, she found her senses and jerked into life.

'Matt! Matt, don't look like that—it isn't what you think, I——'

'No?' he snapped, his face livid under the deep tan. Just what is it, then? Because I can think of only one explanation—and if you can cook up another, you must have a better imagination than I have!'

Jessica scrambled from the bed, thankful that she was still clothed, though the loose shirt and pyjama trousers she'd been wearing ever since Matt had left could hardly be said to be formal. 'Matt, let's go downstairs, I'll explain——'

'And leave lover-boy in possession of the bed? The bed *I'd* hoped to spend the night in?' Matt looked even more incredulous. 'Just what kind of a fool do you take me for, Jessica? And just how insatiable are you? When we made love the other night, I'd have sworn that you hadn't been near a man for months—years, even. Yet the minute my back's turned you've got another one in bed with you—and I suppose if you hadn't fallen asleep you'd have been ready and waiting for me when I got here! My God, I knew when we were married that you were a sexy lady—but I hadn't realised you were a nymphomaniac. And you have the nerve to sit in judgment on *me*!'

'No—no, it's not like that, I told you. Matt, come downstairs——'

'Not before I've thrown this joker out.' Matt ripped back the duvet. 'Why, it's *Chris*! Well, I knew you were friendly, but I thought better of him than this, whatever sort of a slut *you* might be—and what's the matter with him anyway? How the hell can he sleep through this?'

'He's drunk,' Jessica said desperately. 'Matt, it's no good, he won't wake up, you'll have to leave him there.'

'Drunk? Well, you've been having quite a party, haven't you? What is it with you, Jessica?' His grey eyes raked her from head to foot with scorn. 'Can't you manage without it for a few hours? And did you have to get Chris dead drunk before he'd let you have your way with him?' He dropped the duvet back on Chris's recumbent body. 'All right, so he stays. But I don't.' He wheeled round and went down the stairs like a sailor going down a companionway. 'You can't have two men at once, Jessica, even if your perverted tastes do run to it. Not when I'm one of the men, anyway.'

Jessica followed him down and stood helplessly by the door, watching him put on the jacket he had taken off as he came into the cottage. She could think of nothing she could say to prevent him going—nothing that could make him believe her actions innocent. But she couldn't let him go like this—she had to do something! Frantically seeking the right words, she blurted out: 'Matt, please! I didn't mean you to find me like that—I just fell asleep! I forgot you were——' The bitter fury in his eyes silenced her and she cringed away from the anger that seemed to make his body expand before her floundering explanations.

'I just bet you didn't mean me to find you like that!' he said at last, his voice clipped with the iron control he was placing on himself. 'I just bet you didn't. But you *fell asleep*.' The tone of his voice whipped her mercilessly. 'You *forgot I was coming*. If you hadn't insulted me enough already, Jessica, you'd have made sure of it with those few kind words. And they were supposed to make me feel better, were they? Supposed to be some kind of excuse? Well, you'll have to forgive me—I work to a slightly different moral code from yours and to me they don't seem to make things the slightest bit better. Not the slightest bit.'

A sudden surge of indignation took Jessica by surprise, and before she even had time to examine it she had allowed her feelings full rein. Stepping closer to him, she lifted her chin and glared up into his cold grey eyes, her own tawny with anger. She tossed back her tangle of copper hair and clenched her fists as she blazed at him.

'Oh, so you work on a different moral code, do you? Do you really think that's news? Isn't that why we split up in the first place? Because of your moral code—or absence of it? What about all those girls—Fiona, Sylvia Steele and the rest of them? You've been playing around for years, Matt Fenwood, and you think you can pass judgment on me! And you won't even listen— not even when there's a perfectly rational explanation. You won't even give me a chance!'

'And how much chance did you give me?' Matt demanded, his voice dangerously quiet. 'How much explanation was I allowed to give? No, Jessica, the laws have to be the same for everyone or they just don't work. But we'll leave it at that, shall we? Call it quits. If you do have an explanation for tonight's little escapade—one that will hold water—I'll be interested to hear it. But not tonight. I've got better things to do!'

He turned on his heel and wrenched open the door, slamming it behind him with a crash that seemed to shake the whole house and must surely have woken even Chris. Jessica stood quite still, making no attempt to prevent him leaving. It would have been no use, she realised dully. Matt had stormed out of her life as surely and finally as he'd stormed in. This time it really was the end. He would never, never come back again.

Slowly, as if nothing really mattered any more, she went back into the living-room and sank down on the sofa. Whether she slept or not hardly seemed to matter. Life was just something for getting through now; a long, weary vista of years, stretching endlessly ahead.

CHAPTER EIGHT

CHRIS appeared in the kitchen next morning shamefaced but apparently refreshed, which was more than Jessica felt after a sleepless night on the sofa. She looked up from the mug of steaming coffee which was all she could face and decided that there was little point in telling him just what his presence had done to her life; it would mean too much painful explanation.

'Hi,' she said without enthusiasm. 'Feeling better?'

Chris pulled a wry face. 'Since I don't remember much since yesterday afternoon, I can't really answer that question. Probably I do. Jessica, I hope I wasn't a nuisance last night. I know I came here feeling that there wasn't anywhere else to go, and I know you were marvellous—but you can't have been very pleased about it. I'm sorry.'

'Oh, that's all right,' Jessica said untruthfully. 'What are friends for, after all? Chris—what you said about Sue, wanting a divorce. Do you really think she means it? Or would you rather not talk about it?'

Chris sat down and poured coffee into a mug. 'God knows, Jessica. I know I believed her yesterday—why should she say it, otherwise?' He leaned his head on one hand. 'What a mess I've made of everything. What a hell of a mess!'

'Chris, don't give up.' Jessica reached for his hand. 'Look, you and Sue are going through a rough patch—but it doesn't have to be any more than that. You still love her, don't you?'

Chris didn't answer at once; then he gave Jessica a lopsided grin.

'Yes, I do. Oh, Jess, I know I said things the other night about us—but it really is Sue. I'm sorry.'

'Oh, for goodness' sake, you don't have to apologise for *that*!' Jessica brushed his words aside. 'There was never anything deep between us—never could be, while we're both in love with someone else.' She hurried on, conscious of Chris's eyes on her face. 'Look, what I'm saying is this thing between you and Sue could easily go the wrong way, if you let it. Especially if there *is* someone else. *But you don't have to let it.* You and Sue split up just because of your job, didn't you? Because you were away from home so often. Not because there was anything wrong between you.'

'Yes, but I don't see what difference——'

'It means you've got a fighting chance, at the very least,' Jessica urged him. 'Sue loved you—she wanted more of your company, not less. She was lonely because *you* weren't there. And the only reason she's turning to someone else now is because she thinks she's lost you and she's more lonely than ever.'

'So what can I do about it?' Chris gazed at her with perplexed blue eyes. 'We've been over all that. Sue won't move nearer, and I can't get the kind of job I could do well where she is.'

'Well, that's something you've got to sort out between you. But it must *be* sorted out.' Jessica looked at him with a touch of exasperation. 'Chris, don't be so *feeble*! This is your *marriage* you're talking about. You've got to work at it—not just give up at the first hurdle. So one of you has to give in—probably both of you, to some extent. That's what it's all about, isn't it? The good old British compromise.' She finished her coffee and stood up. 'Put some effort into this, Chris. Getting drunk and coming whining to me isn't going to help anyone.' Least of all me, she thought a trifle bitterly. 'Look, once this week is over your part in the film has finished. Can't you take some leave.'

'Yes, I suppose I could,' Chris said doubtfully. 'Actually, before all this blew up we'd talked about having a holiday around Easter. But——'

'Then *do* that,' Jessica told him firmly. 'Go into the travel agency this morning and book up for somewhere warm and sunny, ring Sue up and tell her to get ready and *go*. It's my betting she'll be glad of the chance, and if you can't sort something out between you on a sunny beach in Spain or somewhere, then there's no hope for you!'

'This *morning*? But——'

'Nothing's scheduled till this afternoon,' Jessica said. 'I'm seeing rushes this morning, but you needn't. Just come along when you're ready—it won't take long, anyway—and *don't* come until it's all arranged.'

Chris stared at her and she looked back at him, wondering why her own problems didn't seem so clear-cut. Perhaps she was over-simplifying Chris's. She hoped she wasn't making things worse instead of better.

'All right,' said Chris at last. 'I'll give it a try. I've nothing to lose, after all.' But he still sounded dubious, and Jessica pounced on him.

'Well, don't ring Sue up with *that* sort of voice! She'll turn you down straightaway—I know I would. Positive thinking, Chris. *Tell* her—tell her it's all arranged and you want her to go with you. Tell her you want to try again and you're ready to meet her halfway—even if you don't know how. Tell her you *love* her, for God's sake!'

Chris grinned suddenly and the anxious lines cleared. 'Okay, Jess, you've made your point. I've turned into a bit of a whiner, haven't I? Sorry for myself—I know I was yesterday. And I can see that isn't the way to get Sue back. Faint heart never won fair lady, and all that.'

'That's it,' Jessica smiled. 'Women still like the strong, masterful men, deep down.'

'Even in these liberated days?' Chris asked, smiling, and she laughed.

'Yes—except that in these liberated days men have to be that much stronger again. And it's *real* strength a woman looks for—mental and emotional, not just

physical. The idea that a man could master a woman
just because he was a man and therefore superior has
gone right out of the window. He's really got to be able
to prove it now!'

'Right,' said Chris. 'So off I go to prove it. And I just
hope it works.' He stood up and faced Jessica across the
table. 'Thanks, Jess. You've done a lot for me, you
know that? Even if this doesn't work——' he raised his
hand to ward off her protests . . . '—yes, I know, positive
thinking—and I really am determined to do everything
in my power—but *if* it doesn't work, then at least I'll
know I tried. I won't have given up without a fight.'

'That's it, Chris. And good luck!' She watched as he
left the cottage and walked down the path, his stride
firm. Quite the little marriage guidance counsellor, she
thought bitterly. The only trouble was, she couldn't
manage her own marriage. And there was no one to
come to her rescue as she hoped she had come to
Chris's. Not that it would be of any use, anyway. The
way Matt had stormed out last night had ben very, very
final.

But she could not allow herself the luxury of
wallowing in self-pity, and she'd learned when she and
Matt had first parted that it would only make her feel
worse. There was work to be done: work, the time-
honoured palliative.

Moving more briskly, Jessica washed the two mugs
and put them away. Then she went upstairs, made the
bed and collected her things for the day. Once the week
had started, the time would go quickly, and the sooner
she arrived at the studios and set it all in motion the
better.

Most of the day was to be taken up with rehearsals of
the dramatisation to be filmed that week, but there
would be time before that to see the rushes of last
week's work. Jessica went along to the small room
where she had arranged to see them, passing the piles of
wide, thin cans which contained film and always littered

the corridor. She turned into the crowded office and found a seat, nodding a good-morning to Terry, whose lair this was. He turned off the lights and switched on the machine, and the film began to run.

It seemed to have come out quite well, Jessica thought, watching the documentary sequences. They were not using the sound so she couldn't hear what the interviewees were saying, but they all seemed to be coming across quite well, with few signs of nervousness. And the outdoor and atmospheric shots were fine; she watched with delight as shot after shot came up showing the Welsh mountains in all their rugged beauty. She recalled the names of some of them—Tryfan with its three jagged peaks, Bristly Ridge, Castle of the Winds and, somehow even more evocative of sinister wildness, the Devil's Kitchen. And Cader Idris, the throne of Idris. Who had Idris been? Some ancient chieftain, she supposed, and quite a giant too, to have made a throne out of a mountain.

The door to the little room opened and she glanced over her shoulder to see Jeff Bridger, the cameraman. He nodded at her and she gave him a thumbs-up sign to indicate her approval; then they both turned back to the screen.

Two or three more people came in after that, but Jessica and Jeff were too absorbed to notice as they watched the rushes, slowing the picture down or speeding it up as they discussed the technical points of the filming. On the whole, Jessica thought, it was very good indeed, and if this week went as well as the last, they should have plenty of good material from which to make up their programme.

'The fire scene will be the trickiest, of course,' she observed as the film came to an end and Terry put the lights on again. 'But if we can bring it off it will be fantastic—a real climax to the whole thing, just as it was in the book. Hilary, will you just run through all the details and make sure we haven't forgotten anything.' She glanced at her watch and then looked round at the assembled faces, surprised to see how many had arrived. 'We'll have some coffee now, I think, and then I'll get on with the rehearsals if the artistes are here. And then. . . .' Her voice trailed away as she saw Matt, sitting in the corner of the room. When had *he* come in? And why hadn't some sixth sense warned her that he was there? 'Then we'll look forward to a good week's shooting,' she finished with a note of trembling defiance.

Matt uncoiled himself from his seat. His face was impassive but his eyes were watchful and Jessica knew that there was no warmth in them for her, only an icy aloofness. He looked down at her, then half-turned away and spoke almost over his shoulder.

'Perhaps you'd like to have your coffee with me, Jessica. There are a few things we ought to discuss.'

Jessica stood mute as the others crowded round him with excited questions about his escape from Buwambo. They had all heard about it on the news at the weekend, but they naturally wanted the story from his own lips. Matt, however, fended them off, telling them that he was due to give an interview on the T.V. news that evening and they'd hear it all then.

'It's too long a story to start telling now,' he said. 'It's a busy week for you, and I don't want to hold things up. Jessica?'

The word was spoken as a question, but Jessica knew quite well that it was a command. She glanced round at the others, muttering something about seeing them in twenty minutes or so; then she followed Matt miserably down the corridor, wondering just what it was he thought they had to discuss, and knowing already that whatever it was, he would win.

'Right,' said Matt, closing the door firmly. 'Now let's get one or two things straight.'

'Matt, if it's about yesterday Chris will tell you——'

Jessica began breathlessly but he cut across her words, his voice harsh and uncompromising.

'Then he can save his words. I'm not interested in any fairy stories you've cooked up between you. I'm not interested in yesterday anyway. It's the film I want to talk to you about.'

'The film?' Jessica looked at him, startled. 'But it isn't finished yet, I told you——'

'And *I'm* telling you. It won't do, Jessica.'

'Won't *do*? But it's terrific—and Jeff's camera work is wonderful, it's all coming over exactly as I wanted it——'

'Then that's a pity. I had hoped you would see the faults for yourself—instead, you obviously see them as virtues, and that's why it won't do.'

Jessica shrugged helplessly. 'I don't know what you're talking about.'

'Those interviews,' he said grimly. 'I've seen the transcripts and they're showing a hopeless bias. The whole film is coming down firmly on the side of young Huw and all that he represents. It's quite apparent, even at this stage—and that sound interview with the young man himself clinches it.'

'Well, of course it does!' Jessica clenched her hands as she stared up at him. 'That's the whole point. The film is saying what the book says—that the situation should never have been allowed to arise, that something ought to be done even now to stop it——'

'Like what?' Matt cut in, and she shook her head and spread her hands.

'Like some of the people I've interviewed have suggested. Charging extra rates on holiday cottages, for instance—refusing improvement grants—that sort of thing. Making the ownership of holiday cottages expensive, so that fewer people will buy them in the first place, and those who do will pay more into the community for the privilege.'

'And you really think that would work? Jessica, you

haven't even begun to think about this problem. You've just listened to a lot of fanatics, taken their word for everything and given no thought at all to the problem as it really is. Look—point one. The local people in the Welsh villages *haven't* been in the habit of buying their own homes. Not people like Huw, anyway, young men who were farm labourers, quarrymen or miners. Most of them lived in tied accommodation—cottages provided by the employer. Now a good many of those employments have gone, dwindled away. Mechanisation has cut down the labour force on farms and many of the quarries are worked out, or modern building materials have rendered them defunct. So the workers have gone to the towns. There isn't anyone to *live* in those cottages. If they hadn't been bought by city people as second homes they would have become derelict and disappeared altogether. Isn't it better that they should have some use, give some pleasure? And as for your idea of charging extra rates—they're paying two lots already. Plus the fact that they get very little back from the rates they pay on their cottages. How much do they take from the local authority?—tell me that. No children to be educated, very little rubbish to be disposed of, they don't even use as much water. Have you considered *any* of those things, Jessica?'

'Well, you certainly have,' she retorted. 'And you say I'm biased! Don't you think you are just as much, on the other side?'

'I'm simply trying to *present* the other view,' he said patiently. 'Look, I know as well as you do that it isn't that simple—it isn't black and white. Very few things are. It's probably six of one and half a dozen of the other. But I don't want you presenting either side as twelve. Give it a balance. Get someone on film who will talk about the other points of view. At present, I get the impression that if young Huw were really going to set fire to that cottage you'd be out there passing him the matches.'

And so I would, Jessica thought stubbornly. Aloud, she said stiffly: 'Have you any other instructions before I go?'

'Yes, I have, as a matter of fact.' Matt turned and shuffled through some papers on his desk, and Jessica recognised the pale blue paper on which the script was typed. 'This fire scene—you realise you're going way over the budget if you include it?'

'Yes, and I've tried to economise in other ways. I've cut down as much as I can.' Jessica watched him anxiously. Surely he wasn't going to try to cut that—it was the most important scene of the film. 'I can't get it down any more, Matt, I'm sorry.'

'You can, you know.' His grey eyes were implacable and she knew with sinking heart what he was going to say next. 'You can drop that scene—on film at least. Show it on wildtrack, it'll be just as eff——'

'Wildtrack?' Jessica interrupted. 'Sound only? Matt, you're crazy! That scene's the climax of the whole film—how could it possibly be done on wildtrack? The whole thing would fall completely flat.'

'Not at all. You could do it over Euan's interview. The sounds as he described the way he crept round the cottage; the noise of the flames spreading, wood crackling, tins and bottles in the kitchen exploding. Use a bit of lighting effect too, and it would be——'

'Completely theatrical and a complete anti-climax,' Jessica finished for him. 'No, Matt, it's out of the question. The scene's all arranged and it's going ahead. I'm sorry about the budget, but it simply proves that the budget wasn't realistic to begin with. Maybe you can recoup it from one of the others in the series.'

'And I can just see my other directors agreeing to that!'

'Oh, you know what I mean—maybe their films won't quite reach budget limits. And you know you keep a bit in hand anyway——'

'For contingencies, yes. This doesn't happen to come

into that category. This is a deliberate over-running——'

'For something that's worthwhile!' Jessica turned away and gripped the back of a chair. 'Matt, this film is talking about something important—something that affects people's lives, people who haven't got anyone to speak for them. That's why these fires happen—because they've got no way of telling the world what's happening to them, because——'

Matt cut her short with a gesture of impatience. 'My God, Jessica, you really have soaked it all up like a sponge, haven't you! And I thought you could keep a balanced opinion! Doesn't it occur to you that there may be other factors involved in this—political factors? Haven't you ever heard of infiltrators—haven't you heard of people taking a certain course of action in the knowledge that others will follow them—and they can then sit back and watch the innocents do their dirty work for them?'

Jessica stared at him. 'You surely don't think——'

'I don't honestly know. But isn't it possible? And if it *is* so, aren't you playing right into their hands by making a film like this and positively encouraging others to take the same action?' Matt took a step nearer. 'Jessica, all I'm asking is that you present a balanced view and *cut out that fire scene!*'

He laid his hands on her shoulders, but Jessica wrenched herself away. Her tawny eyes blazed as she glared up at him, and she tossed bronze hair back over her shoulder and almost spat out her words.

'So it's politics now, is it? A minute ago it was the budget! Just what is it that worries you about that scene, Matt? Just what are you so scared of? Maybe it isn't either of those things—maybe it's something quite, quite different. Maybe you're just scared because you can see that I'm making a good film, the best I've ever done, and that wasn't in your scheme of things, was it? You wanted me to make a mess of it, so that you could prove that I'd never make a director. You wanted to make me look a fool and now you can see I'm not going to—not unless I follow your orders, cut the best scene in the film and replace it with some feeble and ineffective wildtrack. *That* would serve your purpose all right, wouldn't it? Well, it won't work—the scene stays in!'

'Jessica, stop being childish. Of course I didn't want to make you look a fool. Do you think I'd play around with the company's money like that—not to mention a skilled crew? I told you what the problem is—the whole thing's getting too political, as well as too expensive. I don't have the final say in these matters, you know— and if this programme upsets the powers-that-be we could all be in trouble.'

'Oh, so it's your *job* you're worried about,' Jessica said scathingly. 'And don't kid me that it's anyone else's—yours and mine would be the only heads to roll if it came to the crunch. And I can't believe that you're worried about mine. Well——' she raised her chin and faced him defiantly, '—let's make the film and see what happens. *I'm* not worried—I was intending to leave Mercia anyway once this job was finished. But if *you're* scared, maybe you'd better take over the direction yourself and make your nice, safe little film with lots of pretty scenery and people in tall hats saying what a shame it all is, look you now, boyo. Then there won't be any danger, will there?'

Pushing past Matt, she made her way to the door, jerking it open. Behind her, he was silent; then, just before she closed it, he said: 'Jessica.'

'Yes?' Jessica said, without turning.

'What did you mean, you intended leaving Mercia T.V.? Is that a recent decision?'

'No,' said Jessica, and turned to face him with contempt in her eyes. 'I decided that a few weeks ago. It was quite obvious that it would be totally impossible for us to work here together. And I can see now that I was absolutely right!'

She shut the door behind her and walked quickly away down the corridor, breathing rapidly. The warmth of her cheeks told her of the angry colour that flew like flags, betraying her agitation, and to her fury she felt close to tears. There was no way she could face the others like this—she needed a few minutes in the ladies' cloakroom to calm herself down.

All the same, she was determined on one thing. The cottage scene would go ahead as planned—and if Matt cut it she would resign on the spot.

To Jessica's relief, the cloakroom was empty when she went in and she was able to give vent to her feelings for a few minutes. But not for long—anyone might come in without warning, and she was determined not to give Matt the triumph of revealing her distress to others. Anger, yes, she had no objection at all to other people knowing she was angry with him—but she didn't want anyone else to see these stupid, maddening tears that insisted on slipping down her cheeks, or to guess at their cause.

Taking a deep breath, Jessica mopped her face and then washed it clean. Luckily she had in her bag the few items of make-up that she used while working, and she was completing her repairs when the door opened and another girl came in. Jessica glanced sideways to see who it was—and froze, the lipstick still half an inch away from her mouth.

'Well, hullo,' Chantal Gordon said in that well-known, drawling voice. 'It's Jessica, isn't it? Matt's ex?'

'Not quite,' Jessica answered, thankful to find that her voice seemed fairly steady. 'Not ex. We're still married.'

'Oh yes, in *name*. But there's no more to it than that, is there?' Chantal said carelessly. 'Just a matter of formality once Matt has time to see to it.'

Jessica seethed. Chantal was taking a lot for granted, wasn't she? And the implied insult—that the ending of

their marriage was so comparatively unimportant,
something to be dealt with when Matt had time! Keep
cool, she advised herself, it's the only way to deal with
women like Chantal Gordon. And she put the lipstick
to her mouth once more.

'Have you come to see Matt?' she enquired politely.
'He's in his office—I've just left him.'

'Yes, we're recording an interview for the News
tonight.' Chantal leaned against the wall, watching
Jessica in the mirror. Her hair fell like a cascade of
platinum to her shoulders, her skin was tanned to a
smooth gold, and her figure, encased in a silvery-blue
suede suit with darker blue suede boots, was superb.
She didn't look a bit like a woman who had trekked
across two African states to escape from revolutionaries.
I look more like that myself, after a row with Matt,
Jessica thought sourly.

'You must be glad to have got him home safely,' she
remarked, wishing that Chantal would go and
wondering why she bothered with this stilted conversation anyway. Why couldn't she just ignore the woman?
But Chantal Gordon wasn't the kind of woman anyone
ignored.

'Oh, I don't know.' Chantal stretched herself
languidly. 'It was rather exciting, actually. And I was
furious at having to leave the excavations just at the
most interesting point. But, that apart—well, if one
does have to be stranded in Africa, one couldn't wish
for better company than Matt! In some ways, I'm quite
sorry to get back.'

And I don't have to enquire too deeply to know what
she means by that, Jessica reflected, unable to help
imagining the ways in which Matt and Chantal might
have kept each other company during their journey. A
sudden longing shook her as she remembered the past
weekend. Yes, Matt would be good company on a trek
through Africa—just as good company as he'd been in
her little cottage. But it hadn't been real, had it—not

for him. It had been just an amusing way of passing a
free weekend, and his fury at finding Chris in her bed
was the frustrated anger of a man who had been
displaced by someone else—no more than that. And
that was something she would do well to remember.

'Actually, I'm rather glad to have this chance to talk
to you,' Chantal said suddenly. 'I've been thinking it
might be quite a good idea for us to get together.
Discuss things—get them sorted out.'

'Things? What things?' Jessica looked at her warily.

'Oh, you know—this divorce. I know it's almost five
years, but I get the feeling Matt would rather not wait
even the last few months. Honestly, we'd both be
happier if we could just have it all out of the way now—
and you wouldn't mind, would you? You've got your
own career and you're not really interested in men
anyway, are you? I understand you haven't even had a
regular boy-friend since you and Matt parted.'

Jessica stared at her. She felt her face flush scarlet
and caught Chantal's amused gaze on her warm cheeks.
Just how patronising could the woman get? Did she
really think she could talk to Jessica like that—as if she
were a child—and get away with it? And the way she
spoke of Jessica's 'career'—as if it were some tuppenny-
ha'penny office job. And not interested in men—what
was *that* meant to imply?

'I think you've got things wrong,' she said coldly.
'Matt and I have never discussed divorce. And if I'd
wanted one I imagine I could have got one quite easily
within the last four years, with or without Matt's co-
operation.'

'But why didn't you?' Chantal asked, opening her
eyes wide. 'You don't *want* Matt—why hang on to him?
Why drag it out all this time? Don't you think you're
being just a teeny bit dog-in-the-manger?'

'I could point out that Matt could have asked for a
divorce at any time,' Jessica retorted, feeling a tremor
somewhere deep inside her. 'He never has. Perhaps he

too had his reasons.' Though to herself, she acknowledged that she hadn't the least idea what they might be. Perhaps it just hadn't been important enough, as Chantal had implied; or perhaps he'd been using Jessica herself as a shield, a protection from other women with marriage in mind.

'Well, he probably will now,' Chantal said smoothly. 'After our experience in Africa—well, we just don't want to waste any more time. I'm sure you understand. So why not be civilised about it? Don't hang on those last few months just to spite him—tell him you'll go along with any arrangements he decides to make. It can all be over very quickly these days, you know.'

'Just like going to the dentist,' Jessica observed cynically. 'I'm sorry, Chantal. I think this is something between Matt and me. And so far he hasn't mentioned the subject.' Not that he'd be likely to while he was sharing her bed! She looked at Chantal again, wondering what the beautiful blonde would say if she knew just what Matt and Jessica had been doing. 'Quite frankly, I wish you joy of him,' she added with a sudden spurt of anger at the way he had treated her. 'One thing I've learned about Matt Fenwood is that he's devious enough to make Machiavelli look like a novice. I wouldn't trust him as far as I can climb Mount Everest!'

But nothing, it seemed, could penetrate Chantal's smooth complacency. She merely smiled maddeningly and said: 'We'll see. Every man needs the right woman to bring out the best in him. Matt needs me—ask him yourself. And while you're at it, have a little talk about the divorce. I think you'll find he's all in favour.' She lifted an elegantly-manicured hand—how *did* she manage to keep her nails that shape?—and glanced at a slender gold watch. 'Have to go now, I'm afraid—Matt must be wondering where I've got to. And we can't keep the News waiting, can we!' She gave Jessica a brilliant smile, her even white teeth dazzling against the golden skin. 'You will think about what I've said, won't you? It'll save trouble all round.'

Jessica watched her go. They had been talking for little more than five minutes, yet it seemed more like hours. And if I hadn't been feeling pretty low when I came in here, Jessica thought ruefully, that five minutes of Chantal's company would have made sure I did when I went out.

She was so complacent, the cool blonde, so sure of herself. So sure of Matt, too. Was it really true that he wanted a divorce from Jessica so that he could marry Chantal? On the face of it, it certainly seemed more than possible. And yet—if it were, would he have spent the weekend with her, making love with a tender passion that she could have sworn was genuine?

Well, perhaps he would at that. Wasn't Matt Fenwood known as a philanderer after all? Wasn't he the kind of man to take pleasure where he could find it—the kind of man who would never pass up an opportunity if it threw itself at him? Just as she'd thrown herself at him on Friday night!

Being Matt's wife needn't stop her from becoming also one of his women. Especially when they'd been separated for four years and she had made no secret of her response to him. It probably made the experience all the more piquant.

Sickened, Jessica put away her make-up and snapped the bag shut. Well, it would never happen again, that was for sure. As far as Matt Fenwood was concerned her barrier was now firmly in place and more impenetrable than the Sleeping Beauty's thorn hedge. It would need more than a prince in the shape of a T.V. producer to get past it.

As for the divorce—well, she'd think about that. It was true that there was little point in hanging on for a few more months just for the sake of it. But she felt little inclination to help either Matt or Chantal just at present. It was more important to get her own life sorted out first. And that meant, in the immediate future, making a good job of this film.

Squaring her shoulders, Jessica made her way to the rehearsal room where the actors and some of the crew were sitting round, drinking coffee and waiting for her. As she entered, they all looked up and she caught the expression of anxiety on their faces.

'Well?' said Jeff, getting up as she came through the door. 'Have you talked to Matt about the fire scene? The rumour is he's killing it—is it true, or do we go ahead as planned?'

Jessica looked round at the circle of faces, some expectant, some resigned as if they already knew the truth. Determination flooded into her. That scene was *right*—she knew it was. It had to be made. The budget—politics—whatever the problem was, it could be sorted out later, but this was one thing she *wasn't* giving way on.

'The scene goes ahead as planned,' she declared firmly. 'Let's start rehearsing right away.'

And put that in your pipe and smoke it, Matt Fenwood, she thought grimly. Next time, choose a director who doesn't have a mind of her own. Or who's afraid to use it if she has.

CHAPTER NINE

JESSICA did not return to the studios that week. Filming was taking place at the derelict cottage on the flank of Cader Idris, and the entire crew was staying in Dolgellau, a few miles away. It was a relief, she thought, to be out of Shrewsbury. Much as she loved the ancient town with its timbered buildings and narrow passages, standing in a broad loop of the River Severn, it had begun lately to affect her in a way that was almost claustrophobic. There was no knowing when she might suddenly run into Matt in one of those dim and twisting passages, and she felt constantly on edge.

Well, once this week was over she could perhaps relax a little. There would still be plenty to do, of course—next week she would be able to see the whole of the film, running to several hours, and then she would have to spend several weeks in deciding exactly what shape the film would take, sorting out the masses of transcripts of both film and sound recordings, matching them with the film itself and doing what was virtually a huge jigsaw without knowing the picture in advance. It was highly complex work and took endless time and patience, but once it was done and the film complete there was a tremendous sense of satisfaction. The main problem was in retaining one's detachment— it was difficult, after becoming so deeply involved with the subject, to look at it objectively.

Rather reluctantly, Jessica considered what Matt had said—was she really allowing her own feelings to cloud her judgment on this film? Would it be just as well to record a few interviews of the kind he had suggested, so that she would have them if she did decide to use them? Possibly when she saw the completed run-through she might feel that it did need balancing—and if she didn't, there would be no harm done. At least he couldn't accuse her of going directly against his wishes—she was already doing that with regard to the cottage, and she didn't want to get the reputation of being a difficult director. Particularly if she were to try to work with another company.

Well, she could get Chris on to finding some more subjects for interview and they could perhaps be fitted in at the end of the week. The fire scene, last of all, was scheduled for Thursday night, leaving Friday free for any emergencies. So far there hadn't been any, and with luck Friday would remain free. Jessica knew that the crew had all hoped for a long weekend, but they wouldn't object if there were any more filming to do; several of them were paid on a piecework basis, as freelances, and unlikely to turn down extra money.

Someone up there likes us anyway, she thought next morning as she drove to the filming site. The sky was pale blue, with flecks of white cloud scattered across it like snowdrops; the coppices on the lower slopes of the mountain were a tender green as the buds opened, and along the banks were clusters of yellow primroses and the occasional patch of purple violets. In some of the fields were lambs, old enough now to leave their mothers for a game together, and Jessica smiled as she spotted half a dozen taking turns to climb on to and leap off a bale of hay. They were actually queueing up, and she wondered for the hundredth time how such an obviously bright and intelligent creature as a lamb could possibly grow up to become a slow, impassive sheep.

The derelict cottage was at the end of a rutted, unmade track, and Jessica bounced the car along it, wondering what state the surface got into after heavy rain. It was fortunate that this was a particularly dry spring, or it might have been impassable by the time the crew had been along it a few times in their large cars.

To everyone's relief, the weather stayed fine for the rest of the week. It was always an anxious time, filming outdoors, particularly for drama when the weather might be vitally important. For these shots, precise weather conditions were not essential, except that it was much nicer to film on a dry, sunny day, but for Thursday night it had to be dry–no one, however fanatical, would try to set fire to a cottage in pouring rain. And as the days passed without change, Jessica found herself first relieved that the weather was keeping fine, then convinced that it must break.

'It can't last,' she said to Jeff. 'Not in Wales!'

Jeff looked at the sky. 'Can't see any signs of change,' he observed. 'Barometer's high, too—I looked at the one in the hotel this morning. I reckon we're going to get away with it.'

'Well, I hope so.' Jessica surveyed the scene thoughtfully. 'Let's just run over the details for Thursday night again. You're going to follow Huw as he comes up the path, right?'

'Not sure about that,' said Jeff. 'Wouldn't it be better to come ahead of him—see his face all the way? Then he can break off and creep round the cottage, checking there's no one there. Otherwise we don't get a look at his face at all.'

'And that's important,' Jessica nodded. 'Yes, we'll do it that way. And we'll need some cutaways too, showing his face as he goes round—can't leave them till afterwards as we usually do, because the cottage won't be there any more! So we'll have to rehearse that scene pretty thoroughly to get it right—once the matches have been struck, it's a one-take job!'

'Yes, but Huw isn't actually going to set fire to it himself,' Jeff pointed out. 'Special Effects will do that. So you can retake that scene if you have to. What you can't retake is Huw watching the fire burn—it'll go pretty quickly once it's started. And we have to remember that there's a moon too, and it'll be in shot.

We can't have it streaking across the sky like Halley's comet.'

Jessica grinned. It was doing her good to talk like this with Jeff. He never patronised her as some of the men might, but talked as with an equal, taking it for granted that her judgment was as sound as his, never forgetting that she was director and had the final say but still ready to raise points that he considered important. As a team, they worked well together.

'Well, I think that's pretty well sewn-up,' she said at last. 'We'll rehearse it on Thursday afternoon while it's still light enough for the actor to see what he's doing, and then we'll rehearse again as soon as it gets dark. Better remind Hilary we'll need some kind of supper as well as lunch that day, and gallons of coffee. Don't want anyone fainting from lack of nourishment! When are Special Effects arriving?'

'In the afternoon, so he'll be able to have a good look at the site and see the rehearsal. I'll get the dolly-track laid as soon as he's arrived. The Fire Service are sending a few men out just before dark too, and they'll make sure the fire's out properly once we've finished— not that we can do much damage right out here.' Jeff looked around the bare hillside. 'Can't imagine why anyone ever built a cottage out here in the first place—a shepherd's hut, I suppose. Must've been pretty bleak at lambing time.'

'Well, they do lamb later out here on the hills. I saw some really tiny ones on the way in.' Jessica glanced at her watch. 'I think we'd better get going again. Make the most of this weather while it lasts!'

By Thursday afternoon the filming was up to schedule and the crew began to prepare for the night scene. There were, in fact, few extra preparations to make; the same lights and cameras as usual would be used and it was really a matter of making sure that everyone was well-rehearsed. The brillance of the lights that were used would make everything else seem even darker, so it was important to know the terrain, and for this reason rehearsals were more meticulous than ever.

David Kilbey, playing Huw, was the only actor involved, but the others stayed on to see the action, keeping well out of the way. The Special Effects man, Keith Hammond, arrived and Jessica showed him the site while Jeff laid the narrow track which would be used for running the dolly on which he set his camera for the shot showing Huw walking towards the cottage. The cars were all parked in a shallow quarry, probably the one from which the stone had been taken to build the cottage, and none of them would be able to get out until the track had been taken up; the Fire Service vehicle would have to park a short way down the narrow lane, but Jeff had already checked that they would be able to reach the cottage with hoses should it be necessary.

By dusk, everything was ready. David had walked along the rutted path, following Jeff riding on his dolly and being pushed by the location assistant, more times than he could remember. He had crept round the cottage mimed the actions of pouring petrol, and stood back to watch a non-existent blaze until he knew every stone that lay in his way. Now, Jessica guessed, he needed a break, and she called to Hilary to hand out coffee and sausage rolls.

'That's fine,' she told everyone. 'It should go very well.' She looked at the faces, lit by the garish light of the huge lamps, and was aware of the brittle tension between them. Everyone knew that this was an important scene, which needed careful handling; they also knew that there had been a dispute between her and Matt as to whether it should be shot at all. A cold shiver rippled across her skin. What they didn't know was that Matt had expressly forbidden the scene—and that she was going directly against his orders in shooting it.

Well, there was no point in worrying about that now.

What she had to do was keep everyone else calm, so that the shooting would be successful—there was no sense in risking everything and then making a mess of it. And if she were to instil calmness in her crew, she had to be calm herself.

'Right,' she said, putting her cup down. 'Let's get into position. The fire people are coming—I can hear the engine. Let's get this scene wrapped up, and then all go and have a nice dinner in Dolgellau!'

The team swung into action. It was too late now to back out, Jessica thought, her heart thudding with nervous excitement as she watched the positions being taken up. Chris was with the firemen, explaining just what was to happen, and Hilary was giving the First Aid box a last-minute check. Behind the fire appliance was a police Panda car, with an interested-looking policeman getting out of it. On the site itself, David was already in position at the end of the dolly-track, with Jeff perched on his seat facing him through the camera. The lights were on, ready, and the boom assistant was holding his long pole with the microphone on the end, alert for the signal from the sound recordist, who was out of sight in the darkness. They would probably record David's approach on wildtrack as well, but that would be done after the scene had been shot.

'Okay,' the sound recordist called.

'Right,' Jeff relayed.

'Action,' said Jessica, almost too quietly for them to hear.

David hesitated for a bare second, then started his walk towards the cottage, face set and purposeful but gait showing his anxiety. The only sound was that of his footsteps crunching on the stones; through his earphones Eddie, the sound recordist, would be hearing his breathing as well on the radio mike. The dolly ran smoothly in front of him, making no noise at all, and then reached the end of the track.

'Cut,' said Jessica.

They did it again to make sure but had to abandon the take because a plane went over. The third time David tripped on a loose stone he'd missed before. The fourth was all right.

'Fine,' Jessica said with a sigh of relief. 'Now the creeping round the cottage scene.'

The track was taken up and attention turned to the cottage itself. Jessica watched, feeling her nervousness return. It was so important to get this scene right, to make a really effective climax. Surely then Matt would see that it had to be done this way. Surely he wouldn't refuse to allow her to use it, out of sheer pigheadedness. All right, it was running them over the budget—but films had gone over budget before, and so long as the cause had been worthwhile and not simply careless accounting, nobody had minded too much. And this *was* worthwhile! He had to see that.

Everyone was in position and ready. As Jeff had promised, the weather was perfect, with a full moon climbing into the velvet sky above the cottage roof. Somewhere a lamb bleated and an owl floated by on silent white wings. The lighting was just right, showing the cottage in just enough dim light to catch the whiteness of David's eyes and teeth as she skulked round the walls. Jessica watched as he went over the ground for the last time, making sure of his way, and then braced herself for the final moment.

'Right,' came Eddie's quiet voice.

'Okay with me,' said Jeff.

'Action,' Jessica ordered, and Jeff's assistant Alec, held the clapperboard in front of the camera and recited the slate and production numbers so that they would be recorded at the beginning of the take.

David began his furtive movement round the cottage walls. Jeff kept the camera turning on him as he moved; everyone remained completely quiet.

David reached the first window and paused, using a flash lamp to peer inside. And then, as he continued his patrol, a new voice broke in on the scene, harsh and angry, startling everyone and turning the blood in Jessica's veins to something that felt remarkably like water.

'Cut!'

There was an instant of astounded silence. At the word, Jeff had automatically cut and now he turned and gave Jessica an astonished glance before whipping round to peer into the darkness. 'What the hell——' David was rooted to the spot in the glare of the lamps, shading his eyes to try to see out. And the whole team, frozen in their various attitudes as the command had rapped out, began to recover and ask each other what was going on.

Jessica didn't need to ask. She couldn't see who was out there in the shadows, but she didn't need vision to recognise the owner of that voice. And she knew now that, subconsciously, she'd been expecting this all along.

'Matt!' she breathed; and then, as anger took charge, more loudly: 'Matt!'

'Well?' he said grimly, striding into the light, his shadow rising behind him like that of a giant and looming up against the sky. 'I thought I'd made myself quite clear on the question of this scene.'

'And I made myself clear,' she retorted, planting her feet apart and facing him in an attitude of defiance. 'This scene is vital and I had no intention of leaving it out——'

'Might I remind you that I'm the producer of this film?'

'And I'm the director!' she flashed back. 'I've always been given a free hand with my other films, the producers have been happy to let me make them in my own way——'

'Then presumably you haven't run over your budget and put a definite bias on what you were filming. I warned you, Jessica——'

'And I took notice! Chris has found some more

people to interview and we're seeing them tomorrow. You needn't worry about the politics, Matt, your job will be quite safe.' She made no attempt to hide the contempt in her voice and saw the tightening of his jaw. 'And now, if you don't mind, we'll continue with this scene. The crew have worked hard today and I don't want to be here all night.'

Matt glanced round. The crew had retreated a little but were still within earshot, their faces displaying various degrees of embarrassment and annoyance. It was seldom that this kind of scene took place on a set; producers chose their directors because they felt them to be in sympathy with the aims of the film they wanted to produce and a dispute such as this was rare. And this had been a particularly happy shoot, with everyone co-operating well and plenty of moments of laughter. Not all shoots went as smoothly; there were often quite a few minor difficulties and clashes of personality, and it was especially galling to find things going so drastically wrong at this stage. Adrenalin was running high and if the scene were to be killed it would result in a good deal of bitter frustration.

'I thought I said——' Matt began, but Jessica cut across his words, her anger lending an edge of sharpness to her voice.

'I know what you said, Matt, and so does everyone else! But we can't kill this scene now—we're halfway through it. And there'd be no point anyway—the money's been spent, don't you see? We've renovated the outside of the cottage, which we had to do anyway for exterior shots, we've got everyone here including Special Effects and the Fire Service, the only thing left to do is set fire to the place, and that's only costing a few gallons of petrol. What's the point of stopping now? All we'd save is the cost of the film, and that's peanuts.'

'So you win? You override everything I've said and go ahead as if the producer's wishes are totally unimportant? Be your age, Jessica—there isn't a producer alive who'd let his director get away with that! The scene's killed, and that's that.'

'Be *my* age?' Jessica exclaimed. 'Why don't *you* be *yours*? You're not trying to save money now, Matt—like I said, it's been spent. What *you're* trying to do is save face—trying to pretend you were right even up to the point of wasting the money that's been spent, more effectively than if you let the shot go ahead. Look, if we go ahead we can get a bloody good scene—even if it is expensive. If we don't, we've still got the expense and no scene. So what's it to be?'

Matt stared at her, his face livid in the blaze of light. She could see the twitch of fury in his cheeks and for a moment the controlled violence in his body was so potent that she took a step back, afraid that he was going to strike her. Then the moment passed; he seemed almost visibly to gather himself together and very slightly relax. Jessica watched him warily, wondering just what he was going to do or say next.

But he didn't say anything. He gave her one last concentrated look, then turned away. He walked out of the flood of light and went over to the cottage, tilting his head back to look up at it. Then he glanced around at the camera, the sound equipment and the waiting crew, and Jessica knew that he was assessing all that she had said.

There was complete silence. Everyone was watching tensely, even the firemen. Everyone was aware of the importance of the moment.

After five minutes that seemed more like eternity, Matt turned and came back to Jessica. His face was still tight with anger, but she could see that he had made up his mind and she stared at him anxiously.

'All right,' he said, and his voice was quiet and controlled. 'You can go ahead with the scene as planned. It's obviously too late to stop it now. But whether we use it or not will be my decision—just as will everything else to do with this film. I intend to be consulted at every stage of the editing, Jessica, and don't forget it. And if I don't like it, then the entire thing will be done again, with a different director.' He gave her a curt nod. 'You'd better get started.'

Jessica bit her lip. Matt was well aware, she knew, of the humiliation he'd just dealt her, and in front of all the crew. He'd treated her like a small child, and that was something she wouldn't be able to forget in a hurry. In fact, it was typical of Matt, she thought as she began with burning cheeks to call the crew together again. Concede victory in such a way that the victor feels as though he's lost. Somehow or other he managed to do it every time.

The rest of the scene was shot, David creeping around the cottage as rehearsed and then, with the aid of the Special Effects man, setting fire to the cottage. The blaze went beautifully, flames licking along the walls where 'Huw' had spread his petrol, and flaring up inside where he had thrown it through the windows. The two cameras went into action rapidly, Jeff's assistant filming the fire itself while Jeff concentrated on 'Huw's' face, catching every emotion in the flickering light. Jessica let them go on as long as she could, knowing that she needed plenty of film to get the best moments. Then, almost reluctantly, she called 'Cut' and the firemen moved in to control the blaze.

'That's it, then,' she announced. 'Thanks very much, everybody, it was great. We can all go back and have a good dinner now.' She went across to David Kilbey and congratulated him on his performance as Huw. 'Your face said everything while you were watching the fire,' she said. 'The whole story there. It was marvellous!'

'Thanks,' he said. 'I must say, it's quite a sensation, setting fire to a cottage. Don't think I'll take up arson, though, it's too wearing on the nerves!'

You can say that again, Jessica thought, smiling at him. Involuntarily she turned to look for Matt, but the scene was now an organised chaos of people shifting equipment, packing cars, and milling about apparently at random while the fireman dowsed the last of the flames. The big lights were now turned off and the ensuing blackness was so deep that she couldn't recognise anyone.

Maybe he'd gone already, she thought with sudden hope. Maybe he'd gone even before the scene had been finished, though that didn't seem very likely. But it would be a relief if he had. She just didn't think she could face him again that night.

The interviews that Chris had arranged went smoothly enough next day, though they were an anti-climax after the week's filming and everyone was relieved when, early in the afternoon, Jessica called a halt and declared that she now had enough. The cameras and sound equipment were packed away, together with the lights and other paraphernalia, and the crew made its way home; most of them in the direction of Shrewsbury, those who lived farther afield straight home without returning to the Mercia T.V. studios.

Jessica had not had time to talk with Chris since Monday, and now she suggested that they should drop in at a teashop in Dolgellau before setting off for home. She needed someone to relax and unwind with, and Chris's undemanding company would be exactly right.

To her surprise, Chris glanced at his watch and shook his head. 'Sorry, Jess. I've got to be on my way.' He grinned a little sheepishly. 'Promised Sue I'd be as early as I could.'

Jessica looked at him, then took in what he'd said. 'Chris! You're back with Sue again? That's wonderful!'

'And all thanks to you,' he told her warmly. 'I did what you suggested on Monday—fixed a holiday, then rang her up and just told her to get ready. It wasn't quite as easy as that—I had to do quite a bit of persuading. But she agreed that we needed to talk, and

where better than a cottage in Portugal, right by the
beach? So we're off tomorrow and I promised I'd get
home as soon as I could today to help get everything
ready.'

'Oh, Chris, I *am* pleased,' Jessica exclaimed, then
added remorsefully, 'But I've never even asked you
about it all week. Honestly, I'm sorry.'

'Sorry? You've no need to be sorry. If it hadn't been
for you I'd still be moping about feeling sorry for
myself and letting it all slip away from me. I'd never
have done anything positive—or not until it was too
late. No, you've been a good friend to me Jess, and I
won't forget it—nor will Sue.'

And you don't realise just how good, Jessica thought,
remembering the way Matt had stormed out of her
cottage after finding her with Chris. There had been no
chance of his believing the truth—even if Chris had
told him. He would simply have dismissed it with that
particularly searing brand of scorn he could summon
up so easily, and Jessica would have been even more
humilated. At the moment, her humiliation regarding
that episode was at least private; she didn't think she
could bear even Chris knowing just what had taken
place that weekend.

She had quite enough to bear after Matt's behaviour
on the site on Thursday evening, she thought, feeling
hot at the memory. How *could* he have spoken to her
like that, in front of everyone? Telling her that he would
be consulted at every stage, that in effect the film wasn't
going to be hers any more. Editing was a major part of
making it and it was a part Jessica normally enjoyed;
highly complex, but rewarding, working with the editor
and discussing each fragment, whether it was an
important addition to the structure of the film, what
point it made, how and where it should be used. The
non-narrative, no-interviewer technique demanded that
every word, every picture should have something
positive to contribute, pushing the story along with every

second. People talking, on or over the film, and pictures that meant something; that was the effect that had to be achieved, and it was hard work but, in the end, highly rewarding.

But if she were not to be allowed to do it—if Matt were to be there all the time, demanding that it be done his way—well, there was just no point in Jessica being there. Because he would win—he was the producer, and in any case he always did win. It was one of the most maddening things about him.

So what was she to do? Struggle on, knowing that every day would bring a fresh agony as she not only had to see Matt but to try to work with him as well? Because nothing had really changed, had it? That powerful magnetism, the physical attraction he had for her, was as powerful as ever, and he would only have to glance at her with those grey eyes that could be as hard as steel one moment and as soft as velvet the next, and she would be helpless again. And she knew that, to him, it would mean nothing. It was just a way of amusing himself—passing the time—using up some of the virile energy that possessed him. Like that weekend had been, as she had finally and ruelly realised when Chantal told her calmly that Matt wanted a divorce.

Oh, it was all such a muddle! And it was going to get worse if Matt carried out his threat of being in on the editing of the film. And as she drove back through the late afternoon to Shrewsbury, Jessica knew that she couldn't cope with it. It would be better to get out now, while she still had a few shreds of self-respect remaining. A month of seeing Matt every day, working with him, suffering his scorn and all the time yearning for his touch, and she would be destroyed.

Get out now, she told herself as she left the mountains behind and came into the flat plans of northern Shropshire. Matt can do the editing, it can be his film if that's the way he wants it. I just haven't got the strength to fight any more.

With a decisive turn of the wheel she entered Shrewsbury and made for the studios. There was no time like the present, and she would tell Matt now, if he were in his office. Or—and she found herself hoping that this would be the case—leave him a note if he were out. Then she needn't go back, ever; she could just pack her things and go away, find another job. Anywhere that was away from Matt.

Jessica's heart thumped as she stepped out of the lift and made her way to Matt's office, She began to wonder if she'd been wise in coming here. Did she really want another row—could she cope with one, exhausted as she was from the filming? Perhaps it would be better if she turned round and went away, without seeing Matt. Perhaps she could just write, and not take the risk of seeing him again.

And what did you tell Chris the other day? she asked herself sternly. Don't be so *feeble*. Matt can't *eat* you, for goodness' sake. All you have to do is remain quite calm and cool and tell him you're handing over to him—tell him you've been called away, tell him anything. In any case, he might not be there.

But of course, he was. And Jessica, opening the door to meet that inimical grey stare, knew that she would have been better this time to let feebleness have its way. Better if she'd turned round and gone straight down again in the lift; better if she'd never come.

'Yes?' said Matt as impersonally as if she were a total stranger, and one he didn't much like the look of.

'I—I've come——' Jessica swallowed and started again. 'I've come to talk to you, Matt.'

'Well, I imagined that,' he responded dryly. 'So talk.'

Jessica gazed at him helplessly. He looked back, obviously determined to give her no help whatsoever. Desperately, she cast around in her mind for words.

'You—you're not making this very easy for me,' she ventured at last.

'Is there any reason why I should?' he enquired coolly. 'I take it you've come to apologise?'

Jessica gasped, '*Apologise*? What for?'

'Well, it might be any one of a number of things,' Matt said thoughtfully, and she felt her fists clench. 'But on balance I should think it's for the fiasco over the filming. You've probably had second thoughts, realised I was right and that you've got yourself into deep water and come in to try to get me to help you out of it.'

'*What?*' Jessica stared at him, too taken aback to answer immediately. Then the indignant words burst out of her like a flood. '*Fiasco*? That filming wasn't a fiasco—though you certainly did your best to make it so, walking in on it like that. And I certainly haven't had any second thoughts—in fact, in any other circumstances I'd be feeling pleased at having done a good job. As for asking *you* to help me out of deep water—I'd sooner drown, thank you very much!'

'Really?' Matt's eyes crinkled with a humourless amusement. 'Well, I should think you'll be getting your wish. That film's a disaster, Jessica, and you know it——'

'I know nothing of the sort! And neither do you— you've seen nothing but a few rushes, you've no idea how it's all going to be put together——'

'But I shall have, shan't I?' he interrupted smoothly. 'Because as I told you last night, I shall be there at every stage.'

'And you'll see to it that it's a disaster, won't you?' Jessica declared bitterly. 'In fact, I wouldn't be surprised if that's what you've had in mind all along. Why you gave me the job in the first place. Yes . . .' She sank down on a chair, staring at him as her thoughts took shape. 'It was another way of hurting me, wasn't it? The most devious, cruel and destructive way you could think of. You never did want me to become a director, did you? It was a threat to your own pride.

And when I did, even though we were separated, you made up your mind to destroy me—and this was the way you chose. You gave me a job directing for you— but you were determined I'd never make a success of it, weren't you? And to make sure, you gave me a controversial subject, one that you knew I'd get involved in, and having led me into your trap you proceeded to close it. Forbade me to shoot the most essential scene and tried to wreck it when I went ahead. And then I *still* made it, and made a good job of it too, you played your last card. You said you'd do the editing with me—and I can't win there, can I? You can edit it in such a way that it *will* be a disaster—and there's nothing I can do about it. My reputation will be down the drain, just as you planned, and I'll be lucky to get a job as a P.A. by the time you've finished with me!'

Matt's eyebrows rose during this speech and he watched her, remaining maddeningly calm. When he spoke, his voice was like thin ice.

'My God—did you really work all that out as you went along? And you call *me* devious! I only wish I were—there are obviously hidden qualities to you, qualities I never recognised, and I thought I new you pretty well. And just how was I to explain this appalling waste of money? My reputation's involved as well, you know.'

'Is it?' Jessica stared back at him, determined not to be taken in by his smoothness. 'I wonder, Matt. Couldn't that be the very reason you came to Mercia T.V. in the first place? I often wondered why you should, when you had your own production company and could have worked anywhere. It seemed such a strange thing to do—come to a little station like Mercia, out in the sticks. But if I'm right, it's all quite clear. You came simply to put me down. I was doing too well—it was time to teach me a lesson. Once you've accomplished that you'll go back to your own company and who's going to care what happened out here, where nobody's ever heard of? No, Matt, I don't think your reputation is going to suffer. You've got me to blame, after all.'

'All right, Jessica,' Matt cut in harshly, 'that's enough. I've heard enough of your fantasies. So I'm the big bad wolf and out to destroy the innocent little Red Riding Hood. Let's take it as read, shall we? I can't be bothered arguing about it, and you're so obviously twisted and distorted about it all in your mind that it would be pointless to try. So why *did* you come?'

'To hand in my resignation from the film,' said Jessica. 'I'm not going on with it, Matt. You want to do the editing—you carry on with it. I'm getting out.'

'Now look here,' he began. 'You've signed a contract——'

'And I'm breaking it. It can't do any more damage to my reputation than you're going to do anyway. Sue me if you like, Matt. Nothing on earth would make me edit that film with you—nothing.' She watched as his mouth tightened with anger, and then she took a deep breath and added: 'And there's just one other thing. The question of a divorce. You can have it as soon as you like, Matt—and if you can't be bothered about *that*, I'll go ahead myself. I think it's time this situation was properly resolved.'

'*Divorce?*' he rapped at her. 'Who said anything about a divorce?'

'Chantal did,' Jessica answered in surprise. 'She seemed to think you'd decided not to wait the last few months—and I imagine she would know.'

Matt's eyes brooded under his well-marked brows. He looked consideringly at Jessica; then he got up and walked round the desk towards her.

Jessica watched him and backed away as he approached, her heart thudding. A prickle ran up her spine. It was time to go, she decided abruptly, but before she could open the door Matt was there, leaning against it, his body as immovable as a rock.

'Oh no, you don't,' he said silkily. 'No running away, Jessica. Now—about this divorce. You say you'll go ahead—on what basis?'

'What *basis*? I don't underst——'

'Yes, you do. To divorce me before the five years are up, you need either my consent or sufficient grounds. So—on what basis?'

'Well, you'll consent, surely?' Jessica's forehead creased with disbelief. 'You *want* a divorce—you want to marry Chantal. Don't you?'

'We won't bring that into it, if you don't mind,' he said curtly. 'Just stick to the point. If you don't get my consent—what then?'

'Oh, don't be so naïve, Matt,' Jessica snapped, her patience giving way. 'I've got grounds to divorce you a dozen times over if I care to look. All those items on the gossip pages—all those women! Aren't they sufficient grounds? I wouldn't have any trouble at all, and you know it.'

'No?' he said softly. 'And what about last weekend? Didn't you know that you've only got to spend one night with me to wipe all that out? And we did a little more than spend a night together, didn't we, Jessica my sweet? As I recall, it was practically a whole weekend.'

Jessica's eyes widened. 'You wouldn't!' she breathed, her throat dry with horror.

'Wouldn't I? You underestimate me, dear Jessica. Dear *wife.* If you want to divorce me now, without my consent, you'll have to wait another five years. Counting from last Sunday.'

'No! *No*! I don't believe it.'

Matt shrugged and turned away. 'Don't, then. Ask a solicitor.'

'But—but why?' she whispered, her hand at her throat. 'Why don't you want to finish with it? You want to marry Chantal—she wants to marry you. She's not going to wait another five years, and she's not going to like your reasons for waiting either. I just don't understand.'

'You don't?' Matt turned back and his eyes were dark now with some unfathomable emotion. 'You don't understand?' There was a pause while he looked at her, then he turned away again. 'No, you don't, do you? You never have. Well, we'll have to leave it at that, won't we, and just wait until you do.'

Jessica shook her head. 'You're mad! You're obsessed. Obsessed with yourself—obsessed with being Matt Fenwood. You want everything, don't you, and once you've got it you're not going to part with it, whether you want it or not. That's what it is. You owned me once—or thought you did—and you're not going to let me go. That's why you came last weekend and made love to me—because as far as you're concerned I'm one of your belongings. You don't really want me—but you're going to make darned sure that nobody else has me!'

'Well, I didn't make much of a success of it, did I?' Matt blazed suddenly. 'You hardly let the bed cool before getting another man into it!' He paced away from her, his body trembling, then wheeled back. 'Not want you? I wish to God I *didn't* want you! Life would be much simpler that way.' Before she could move, he had taken her by the shoulders and jerked her towards him; and before she could do more than gasp out a plea for mercy, his mouth was on hers in the most savage, brutal kiss she had ever experienced.

Jessica hung in his arms, utterly powerless to move in that iron grip. He had drawn her up against him so that her feet barely touched the ground, and she could feel every hard contour of his body. Almost involuntarily, her own arms came up and she clutched at his sleeves, trying ineffectually to loosen that inexorable grasp, but Matt only tightened his hold so that the breath was punched out of her body and her lips parted under his. At once, he had taken possession, his mouth invading the moist softness, his hands moving demandingly over her body, seeking out the most sensitive spots.

Jessica whimpered and squirmed in his arms, knowing that it would take only seconds for him to overwhelm her completely; but there was no mercy for her this time, and her movements only served to inflame Matt all the more.

There was still no tenderness in his touch as he carried her to the low chairs at the side of the room, kicking them together to form a makeshift couch. He flung rather than laid her upon them and then stood looking down at her with an expression of sardonic triumph as he began to unbuckle his belt.

Jessica trembled uncontrollably but, although she struggled to get up, the weakness that always invaded her body when Matt touched her turned her legs to jelly and she fell back again. Matt gave a short, unpleasant laugh and dropped his belt on the floor; and she closed her eyes and turned her head away.

'And now,' Matt said silkily, 'let's see if we really want that divorce, shall we?'

CHAPTER TEN

RESTLESSLY, Jessica paced the living-room of the flat. She seemed to alternate these days between bursts of nervous energy and sheer exhaustion, neither of them comfortable to live with and invariably occurring at the wrong times. For instance, this afternoon a bout of exhaustion would have been much more convenient; outside the rain lashed down, there was nowhere to go and she was alone for the next seven hours until Roberta came back. It would have been much better if she could have simply flopped on the big, comfortable sofa and stared at the walls, as she'd done on other days. Instead, she was finding it impossible even to sit down.

She roamed across to the window and stared out at the sodden trees of the park. The fine spring weather had broken since she came to London and the rain had been more or less incessant. It had a very dampening effect on her already low spirits, and several times she had wondered if she'd been wise to come. But she just didn't have the energy to move on again—not for a while, anyway. And Roberta was a good friend, never prying or asking uncomfortable questions but there ready when Jessica did want to talk.

Perhaps she ought to have done what Roberta had suggested today, go along with her to the theatre where she was playing, see the matinee and then have a meal together before the evening performance. But when Roberta had left at lunchtime Jessica hadn't had the strength to go with her; it was only afterwards that this unwanted energy had taken possession of her and set her pacing miserably about the flat.

Things couldn't go on like this, she thought, arriving at the window again. She would have to do something

positive—find work, find somewhere to live, cut all her
ties with Shropshire and begin again. But the enormity
of the task was just too much to face at present. She
couldn't even think straight, and she wasn't even sure
that she'd ever be able to again.

She thought back to the day she'd arrived at the flat,
amazed that it could be only three weeks ago. It had
been lucky that she'd had Roberta to run to. They'd
known each other for years, ever since Jessica's early
days with the B.B.C. She had been assistant P.A.,
working with Maggy Payne on a play, and Roberta had
been a nervous young actress doing her first T.V.
Nerves and inexperience had been a common bond
between the two, and they had become firm friends and
remained so ever since.

Roberta was now a fairly successful actress, keeping
steadily in work without being a household name. Her
present play had been running for nine months and as
she had been unable to leave London much during that
time, she had been delighted when Jessica had arrived
unannounced on that drizzly Sunday evening, dragging
her in and chattering at the top of her voice before she
noticed Jessica's face.

'Jess! What on earth's the matter? You look
terrible—are you ill or something? And I've been
nattering on about myself—here, come and sit down
and tell Auntie Rob all about it.'

'Thanks, but I'm all right really.' Jessica set down her
cases. 'Just had a rather miserable time lately as well as
working hard on a film. Is it all right for me to come,
Roberta? Can I stay?'

'Well, of course.' Roberta glanced at her and asked
no more questions. 'Look, I was just about to get
myself some supper. What would you like? Chicken?
Omelette? Cheese? There's not much else, I'm afraid,
but if you're really famished we could go out.'

'No, that'll be fine. Whatever you were going to
have.' Jessica sat down and leaned her head back. 'I'm

really too tired to care very much, but I know I need something.'

Roberta looked at her again and then went to get the meal. They ate in silence at first; and then, relaxed by food, warmth and two glasses of wine, Jessica told Roberta haltingly what had been happening to her during the past weeks.

Not what had happened on that last evening in Matt's office though. She would never be able to tell anyone about that.

'Well, you can stay here as long as you like,' Roberta said eventually. 'Unless you intend going back . . .?'

'No.' The word came out more firmly than Jessica had intended, and Roberta raised her eyebrows slightly.

'That sounds definite enough, anyway. So what are you going to do?'

Jessica shrugged wearily. 'I honestly don't know. Get another job, I suppose. Try another T.V. company. I can't really think about it at the moment.'

'No, all right.' Roberta tipped the last of the wine into Jessica's glass. 'Well, I'll be glad of your company until you can. Pity about Matt, though. I always thought he was rather a dish.'

'So did I,' Jessica said soberly, and picked up her glass. 'But we live and learn.'

Since that evening she had to all intents and purposes settled in at the flat. After the first few days when she had found herself oddly reluctant to leave its shelter, she had begun to go out with Roberta, wandering round the shops in the mornings, walking in the park, going to see the play. Alone in the evenings, she had inevitably found herself watching T.V.; but she had avoided any programmes which might remind her of Matt and had spent more time reading than viewing.

And, more often than not, she had ended up doing neither but simply gazing blindly at the walls and reliving the weeks since Matt had come back into her life.

She still hadn't worked out just why he had done so. It had been quite deliberate—that was clear—but she couldn't imagine what he'd hoped to achieve by it. Had his plans really been as devious as she'd believed on that last evening—had her accusation been truly accurate? It seemed impossible that Matt could be so cruel—yet she had certainly hurt his pride when she had left him four years ago, and maybe that was something he just couldn't forgive, something he had to punish. It was a side of him that she had never suspected, a darkness in his character that made her shiver.

And that last evening—just what had happened then? She remembered they way he'd flung her on to the chairs he'd kicked together, the way he'd gloated over her as he unbuckled his belt. Jessica had felt more terrified then ever before. Whatever he meant to do to her, it would be done in harsh anger with an added cruelty that made her shake at the thought of it. And there was nothing she could do to stop him. No amount of pleading would move him now; she had never seen quite this determination in his eyes before, but she knew that it denoted a ruthless implacability that nothing would sway.

Matt dropped his belt. He stared down at her, his eyes moving slowly over her body, and Jessica knew that he was mentally undressing her. She wanted to close her eyes, turn away her head, but she couldn't; his gaze was on her like a magnet and she was almost afraid to break the contact.

And then he moved, so suddenly that she was startled into crying out. Instantly, his lips were on her mouth, silencing them with another cruel, bruising kiss, and his hands were moving rapidly and unfumblingly over her body, unfastening buttons and zips, wrenching her clothes away to expose the smooth skin beneath. He held her naked in his arms, his fingers hard and merciless as he sought out the sensitive spots that he had touched with such tenderness less than a week earlier.

Feebly, Jessica tried to push him away, even using legs and feet in her struggles, but she knew at the outset that it was useless. Matt's strength and determination far outweighed her own, and to her dismay she knew that her body itself was betraying her, and harsh as Matt's treatment of her was, it was already softening in his iron grip and moving in response to his demands.

It was all over very quickly. There was no gentle teasing to arousal, no sensuous overture. They came together in a frenzy, no longer sure whether they were fighting or loving, and Jessica clung with fingers, arms, legs and teeth as Matt thrust himself into her with a cry that was almost primitive. The whole world seemed to explode around them; a spasm of fire licked through Jessica's body; she was dimly aware of a roaring noise in her ears and Matt's rapid breathing close to her cheek. And then he had dragged himself away with a wrench that made her gasp, and was sitting on the end of the row of chairs, his head in his hands.

Jessica sat up and touched him with a tentative hand. 'Matt?'

'Oh God,' he groaned, 'what is it about you, Jessica? Are you some kind of witch? Why do you have this effect on me, for God's sake, why?'

'I—I don't know what you mean,' she faltered, still shaken from his rough handling and the shattering climax.

Matt turned and stared at her, and she was shocked to see how haggard he had become in less than half an hour.

'No, I don't believe you do know,' he said at last. 'I don't believe you ever did. Oh—get to hell out of here, Jessica, will you? Just get out!'

'But—Matt, I——'

'I said get out!' he snarled, and thrust her clothes at her. 'I mean it, Jessica—get out, before I do something I'll be really sorry for!'

Bewildered and frightened, Jessica scrambled into her clothes. Matt had buried her face in his hands again and didn't look up as she made for the door. Keeping it half open, she glanced back uncertainly; and then, as Matt raised his head again, she fled.

Rather to her surprise, she had slept all that night and well into Saturday. Shaken and exhausted, it was as if only sleep could keep away the dark memories, and she woke on Saturday only long enough to give the cottage a desultory clean, pack her clothes and force down a meal before going back to bed and sleeping through the night again. On the Sunday, she had locked up the cottage and left for London.

And since then she had spent her time recovering. At least, she supposed she was recovering. Time had smoothed out the worst of the creases in her forehead, had calmed her shivering body and put three weeks of day-to-day living between her and that ghastly evening. But whether she would ever really recover, deep inside—that was another story.

Still unable to settle, she went out into the kitchen and made herself a mug of coffee. She wondered if she drank too much coffee—wasn't it supposed to be bad for the nerves? But it was the only thing she could enjoy these days, her appetite had completely gone, and at least if she made it with milk she was getting some nourishment. Not that it really mattered; nothing really mattered. . . .

The shrill note of the doorbell sliced into the silence and Jessica started, spilling some of her coffee. She put it down on a low table, wondering who the caller could be. Roberta's friends all knew that she was playing matinees on Thursdays. It must be some salesman, or perhaps someone wanting to leave a parcel for one of the other flats.

Pushing her coppery hair back to lie loose on her shoulders, Jessica went to the door and opened it—and stepped back with a shock of dismay.

'Good afternoon, Jessica,' Matt said quietly. 'May I come in?'

His voice jerked Jessica into action. With a quick movement, she pushed the door shut—but Matt was too swift for her. He thrust hard against it, stopping her efforts with an almost casual ease, and shouldered his way into the room. Only then did he allow the door to close, although by then Jessica would much rather have kept it open, and he towered over her, his brooding face set and purposeful.

'Matt?' Jessica said faintly, and backed away from him.

'It's all right, Jessica,' he said abruptly. 'You don't have to worry. I'm not going to rape you again.'

Again, Jessica thought. But that wasn't rape—it was something quite different. An explosion that had had to happen sometime. Trembling a little, but doing her best to keep calm, she sat down on the edge of one of the armchairs.

'Why have you come here, Matt? And how did you know I was here?'

'Roberta told me. All right——' he raised his hand across Jessica's exclamation '—I know you swore her to secrecy. But she happens to be worried stiff about you, and she's got enough sense to know that this is something we've got to sort out between us. She rang me last night and asked a lot of questions, an eventually she told me you were here.'

'But—but she suggested I go to the matinee with her this afternoon,' Jessica said, bewildered. 'She must have changed her mind——'

'Well, I don't suppose she knew I'd come straight-away,' Matt answered reasonably. 'Anyway—I didn't come to talk about Roberta. I came to talk about us.' His eyes moved over Jessica's face and body. 'You're looking like death warmed up, Jessica, and I'd guess you've lost nearly a stone in weight. What in hell's name have you been doing to yourself?'

'Nothing. I'm quite all right—just tired. 'And I needed to lose that weight——'

'Like hell you did! You know I've never gone for the broomstick look.' Matt came forward and sat in the chair opposite.' Jessica, I think it's time we had a real talk and sorted out this mess.'

'Don't you think it's too late for that? Don't you think we've said more than enough already?

'We've said plenty, yes—but none of the right things. We've never really *talked*, Jessica—only quarrelled. Or made love. Or——' He bit off what he had been going to say and his eyes clouded. 'We can't spend the rest of our lives like this. Surely you agree with that?'

'So let's make a clean break,' said Jessica. 'Finish it now. It's the best way, Matt. We were both all right until you came back.'

'Were we?' He looked at her with brooding eyes. 'Were we really, Jessica?'

'Yes, of course,' she said quickly, damping down memories of lonely, yearning nights and a hunger that nothing would assuage. 'I was doing fine as a director, and you've made a big name for yourself. Of course we were all right.'

'And that's all that matters,' he said quietly. 'Work—making a name—being well-known. Do you really believe that, Jessica? Is that really all that matters?'

·Jessica didn't reply at once. There was something new about Matt tonight—some difference in the quality of his voice, in his eyes, that told her he was in desperate earnest. There could be no stone-walling, no evading the issue. Truth was the only communication between them now.

'No, it's not all that matters.' she said in a low voice. 'It never was, though you may not believe that. I just needed to fulfil my own capabilities. Everyone needs that—but not everyone manages it.'

'You mean not every woman. You mean that once a

woman gets married her husband demands priority—his job comes first, is that it?'

'Not in all cases,' Jessica answered steadily. 'But in ours—yes, I do think that's what happened.'

'But don't you see,' he urged, leaning forward, 'I only ever wanted to protect you, Jessica. I knew what a tough world it was, I knew you could get hurt—and the idea of you getting hurt was something I couldn't take. Was that so wrong? Was it so unnatural?'

'Not unnatural, perhaps.' Jessica raised her eyes to his. 'But it was wrong, Matt. Wrong for me. Getting hurt's all a part of life—and I need to live. I've got to be strong enough to take the knocks in order to get the satisfaction of doing what I want to do—and with you wrapping me in cotton-wool there wasn't any way I could develop that strength.'

'But you have developed it, haven't you?' Matt observed, watching her intently. 'I've seen you working and you're tough enough in your job. You didn't go under.' He paused. 'You can still be hurt, though, can't you—away from work?'

'Yes, I can.' Jessica felt as if she were exposing her soul as she said that, but there was no hiding the truth. 'You've hurt me, Matt—you've hurt me a lot. And I still say it would be better if you'd never come back.'

'Yes. I can understand that.' His gaze fell to the floor for several moments, then he looked up and said almost expressionlessly: 'What would you say if I told you I came back because I wanted us to start again.

Jessica stared at him. He was watching her almost anxiously, his eyes no longer veiled. The hardness that the years had brought to his features, dropped away, leaving him looking younger and oddly vulnerable. A sudden unbearable tenderness washed over her and she wanted to kneel beside him, brush back the dark hair that fell across his forehead and kiss away the anxiety.

But the caution born four years ago held her back. Could this be another trick—another way to get her into his arms, to make the situation even worse? And anyway, he'd said *talk*—so talk was all they'd do.

'You wanted us to start again?' she repeated. 'But you never gave a sign—you never even hinted——'

'And would you?' he asked. 'After four years, would you lay yourself open to the kind of rebuff I half expected? I had to see how the land lay first. I had to see if there was any chance at all. That's why I gave you the film to direct—that and the fact that I knew you'd make a good job of it. And I thought it might prove to you that I had faith in your work.'

'I couldn't make out why you'd given it to me,' Jessica confessed. 'I thought you were waiting for me to make a hash of it, so that you would say I told you so.'

Matt sighed. 'Nothing like that. But you were so much on the defensive, I thought there'd be no way of getting through to you. That's why when I went to Africa with Chantal I—well, gave her the wrong impression. It meant nothing really, nothing at all. But I was too stupid to see that myself until we got caught in that revolution. And when we were walking out, scared all the time that the insurgents would track us down, I could think of nothing and nobody but you—you and the thought that maybe I'd never see you again. You—and all I'd lost, all the time we'd wasted.'

Jessica kept her eyes on his face as he spoke, and as his voice faded into silence she knew that he had told her the simple truth. Tears welled in her throat as she gazed at him, and she remembered how she had haunted the newsroom and clung to the radio during that horrific time.

'And when I got back to England the first thing I did was come to you.' Matt looked at his hands as they both recalled that joyous reunion. 'I thought then that the revolution had achieved what I could never have done—shown you what your own true feelings were. You can imagine how I felt when I came back and found Chris in your bed.'

'Yes, I can,' Jessica said simply. 'But Matt, it wasn't what you thought, I can exp——'

'You don't have to. I know what happened that evening.' Matt glanced at her, his expression rueful. 'I ran into Chris and Sue the other day. They'd just got back from their holiday and they both looked radiant. And Sue told me just what had happened that night.'

'*Sue* did?'

'That's right. Chris had told her all about it—but being a woman she'd added two and two together and caught on to what else had happened. She didn't know it all, of course, but she had a pretty good idea that I must have found him there and that our apparent reconciliation—which half the studio had evidently been expecting—had been wrecked by it. She's a sharp girl, that one. Chris is a lucky man.'

'Well, I'm glad things are working out for them,' Jessica said. Then, 'But I did tell you the truth, Matt. You wouldn't believe me.'

'No, I know. The circumstancial evidence seemed too strong.' There was a moment's silence and then he added: 'You wouldn't believe me, either. About Fiona—and Sylvia Steele—and the others. None of it was true, Jessica. It was all just gossip. Once it begins it's impossible to stop and every innocent outing is meat for the columnists. There was never anyone for me but you.'

The tears came to her eyes now, brimming over and slipping silently down her cheeks. So it had all been for nothing, four wasted years. 'Oh, Matt,' she said, 'I'm so sorry.'

He shrugged. 'Well, I guess we've both learned something. 'You've learned what it's like to be held guilty of something you never did, and I've learned that things aren't always what they seem. And I'm more at fault because I already knew that—from bitter experience.' His eyes met hers, grey and steady as rock. 'Well, Jessica? Where do we go from here—if anywhere? Is there any chance for us? Can we start again?'

It was as if the whole of London's traffic had been brought to a halt. Inside the flat it was almost quiet enough to hear Roberta's plants grow; outside there was nothing but a gentle hiss of rain on the windows. Not even the ticking of a clock broke the tension.

'Can we?' Matt repeated, his voice urgent. 'I've got to know, Jessica. These last four years have been hell— loving you, wanting you and trying all the time to fight it. Knowing that nothing, no one could help me forget you and the magic we had together. It was only when I realised what the fifth year meant—that I could lose you for ever—that I had the courage to come back. And even then I couldn't tell you the truth—I had to beat around the bush, trying to make it all happen naturally when of course it couldn't. And instead, I just made things worse—and maybe I've lost you for good this time. Only for God's sake, tell me!'

'Matt, don't!' Giving way at last, Jessica slipped to her knees and cradled him against her, fingers tangling in the thick hair, lips against the rough cheek. 'Of course we can start again—of course it's all right. Don't flay yourself like that—it was my fault, all of it, I should have trusted you——'

'I didn't really encourage you to, did I?' he muttered. 'I could have stopped those rumours if I'd wanted to, in the early stages. But I didn't. I thought they might make you think again, make you do what I wanted and come with me on all my jobs. Only it all got out of hand.' He lifted his head and looked deep into her eyes. 'Jessica, the other night—I felt like hell after that. After what I did to you. I wouldn't have blamed you if you'd never wanted to see me again. I just—well, I just lost control.'

'I know,' Jessica said gently.'It's all right.' And she gathered him close against her again.

For a long time they sat quietly together, saying

nothing but holding each other close. This wasn't a moment for passion, Jessica realised; that would come later. Their relationship would always be passionate and often stormy, but it would be infinitely satisfying. And it would include many more times like this; times when they could sit close, holding each other with tenderness and love, listening to the rain on the windows and knowing that this was the way life was meant to be.

At last the evening began to draw in and the light dimmed. Outside, street lamps shed a golden light and there were sounds on the stairs as other flat-dwellers began to come home. Jessica stirred in Matt's arms and looked smilingly into his face.

'Hungry?' she murmured, and he nodded. 'There's some pâté in the fridge, and I've got a feeling there's a steak. Are you *quite* sure Roberta didn't know you were coming?'

'Whether she did or not,' he said, 'I could certainly eat it. But will there be anything left for her own supper?'

'Oh, I expect so. She can always open a tin of beans,' Jessica said callously. She turned her head and looked at Matt with dancing eyes. 'By the way—there's just one thing you haven't mentioned.'

'And that is?'

'The film. What's happening to it after all?'

'The film?' Matt drew her close again. 'Well, I was saving that. It's fine, Jessica. I've seen the rushes and they're full of good material. You'll make a good programme of that.'

'But—but haven't you begun work on it? And what about the fire scene—and the budget?'

'I haven't done any work on it,' Matt said soberly. 'I just couldn't face it. But the fire scene's terrific just as you said it would be. And as for he budget—well, there are no problems there, one of the others came out quite a bit cheaper than expected. We can scrape it together somehow.'

'Oh, that's wonderful!' Excitement lit Jessica's hazel eyes. 'And I can do the editing? Oh, Matt—Matt!'

'And I thought I was more important to you than your work,' he said ruefully. 'But after this, Jessica, I warn you I intend to have my way. From now on, we work together. Not on Mercia T.V.—we're starting afresh. I've got my own production company and it's going to be big. And you are going to be my first director—is that clear?'

'Quite clear, Matt,' she said demurely. 'And now shall the little woman get your supper?'

'Yes, if she doesn't want to be eaten alive herself. And then——' he pulled her close and Jessica gasped at the contact '—then we'll go to bed. I've a feeling we could both use an early night!'